P9-BYW-791

Hawk's emotions were still all in a jumble and he was at a loss how to sort everything all out.

"I thought that Grayson...I was afraid that you..."

None of this was coming out right.

"Damn it, Carly," he all but exploded, thinking of what *might* have happened to her. "I don't like you taking these kinds of chances."

"You don't have the right to tell me not to do this, you know," she reminded him.

"I know," he answered," but just thinking that something could have happened to you—"

Hawk couldn't bring himself to finish his sentence. Instead, he abruptly pulled her into his arms and kissed her. Kissed her hard, as if there was no tomorrow because, for all he knew, there wasn't one.

* * *

"Like" us on Facebook at
www.facebook.com/RomanticSuspenseBooks
and check us out at www.Harlequin.com!

Dear Reader,

Come with me to a little town called Cold Plains, Wyoming, where everything is perfect...or is it? Beneath its gleaming exterior are dark secrets and an even darker heart at work to turn this once rough-and-tumble town into a gleaming metropolis. But to what end?

This question is what brings FBI special agent Hawk Bledsoe reluctantly back to the town he'd left behind ten years ago. Left behind because Carly Finn, the girl he'd loved, suddenly told him she didn't love him. Through a strange twist of fate, they have to join forces to unlock the secrets holding the town prisoner and save her younger sister. All this while trying *not* to fall in love again.

I hope you enjoy this first installment of Perfect, Wyoming. As ever, I thank you for reading, and from the bottom of my heart, I wish you someone to love who loves you back.

Marie Ferrarella

Watch out for these other books in the riveting new Perfect, Wyoming miniseries:

Rancher's Perfect Baby Rescue by Linda Conrad—February 2012
A Daughter's Perfect Secret by Kimberly Van Meter—March 2012
Lawman's Perfect Surrender by Jennifer Morey—April 2012
The Perfect Outsider by Loreth Anne White—May 2012
Mercenary's Perfect Mission by Carla Cassidy—June 2012

MARIE FERRARELLA

Special Agent's Perfect Cover

ROMANTIC
SUSPENSE

If you purchased this book without a cover you should be aware
that this book is stolen property. It was reported as "unsold and
destroyed" to the publisher, and neither the author nor the
publisher has received any payment for this "stripped book."

Special thanks and acknowledgment to Marie Ferrarella for
her contribution to the Perfect, Wyoming miniseries.

Recycling programs
for this product may
not exist in your area.

ISBN-13: 978-0-373-27758-2

SPECIAL AGENT'S PERFECT COVER

Copyright © 2012 by Harlequin Books S.A.

All rights reserved. Except for use in any review, the reproduction
or utilization of this work in whole or in part in any form by any
electronic, mechanical or other means, now known or hereafter
invented, including xerography, photocopying and recording, or in
any information storage or retrieval system, is forbidden without
the written permission of the publisher, Harlequin Enterprises Limited,
225 Duncan Mill Road, Don Mills, Ontario M3B 3K9, Canada.

This is a work of fiction. Names, characters, places and incidents are
either the product of the author's imagination or are used fictitiously, and
any resemblance to actual persons, living or dead, business establishments,
events or locales is entirely coincidental.

This edition published by arrangement with Harlequin Books S.A.

For questions and comments about the quality of this book
please contact us at Customer_eCare@Harlequin.ca.

® and TM are trademarks of Harlequin Books S.A., used under license.
Trademarks indicated with ® are registered in the United States Patent
and Trademark Office, the Canadian Trade Marks Office and in other
countries.

www.Harlequin.com

Printed in U.S.A.

Books by Marie Ferrarella

MARIE FERRARELLA

This *USA TODAY* bestselling and RITA® Award-winning author has written more than two hundred books for Harlequin Books and Silhouette Books, some under the name Marie Nicole. Her romances are beloved by fans worldwide. Visit her website at www.marieferrarella.com.

To
all the wonderful readers,
who give me
such a great audience
to write for.
You make it fun.

Prologue

Micah Grayson wasn't sure what had possessed him to turn on the TV in the pristine, upscale hotel room that he was occupying for the day. He wasn't exactly the kind of man who craved company or needed to fill the silence.

Hell, in his particular chosen "line of work," silence and stealth were two of his best tools. He had no desire to listen to music or watch anything that might be on the big screen TV that came with the price of the first-class room. For that matter, he only kept up on world affairs insofar as to learn about what region of the world he'd most likely be going to next.

But after methodically going through his own mental checklist and making sure that the room was clear of bugs—not the kind with legs but the kind that could get a man killed—he'd absently switched on the set and sank down on the bed, thinking about his next move.

The grim voice of the newscaster didn't even penetrate his consciousness.

Not until her picture was flashed on the screen.

Very little caught Micah off guard these days. His life was literally riding on this fact, that he was always prepared for any and all contingencies and could act accordingly.

But seeing her face knocked the wind out of him. More than that, it was as if he'd just been on the receiving end of an iron fist aimed straight for his gut.

Because according to the newscaster, the woman in the photograph was dead. And when he had last seen her, a million years ago, before life had gotten so immensely complicated and they had gone their separate ways, Johanna had been very much alive.

Alive, but no longer his.

"In keeping with what seems to have become a bizarre ritual, the body of Johanna Tate was found yesterday outside of Eden, Wyoming. The victim suffered a single gunshot wound. The coroner has concluded that that was the cause of death. This is the fifth such female body found in as many years. Police are asking anyone with any information about this latest murder victim to please step forward. Any informant's identity will be kept strictly confidential. Rumor has it that this young woman was a resident of Cold Plains, a town located some eighty miles away, but this has not been confirmed yet."

A resident of Cold Plains.

Yes, she was from there, Micah thought, bitterness filling his mouth like bile.

As had he once been.

Johanna had been the reason he'd remained in that godforsaken blot on the map for as long as he had. And ultimately, she'd been the reason why he had abruptly left without so much as a backward glance. Because after being his, after planning to share all her tomorrows with him, she'd allowed herself to be charmed away from his side by the very devil himself.

Charmed away by Samuel Grayson.

Never mind that Samuel was his twin brother. He and that underhanded, despicable excuse for a human being were as different as night and day. *He* had never pretended to be anything but what he was, never made any excuses for himself. While Samuel wove elaborate tapestries made of intricate lies to ensnare those he wanted to own, to control for his own unstated purposes.

Crossing to the TV monitor, Micah Grayson turned up the volume.

But the story was over. The dark-haired newscaster had gone on to talk about the unseasonably warm April weather, exchanging inane banter with an overly ripe, barely legal-looking weather girl sporting a torrent of blond hair that appeared to be almost longer than her dress.

Johanna had been allocated less than a sound bite.

Micah hit the off button. The screen on the wall went instantly dark as it fell into silence.

"Damn it, Johanna, I told you he was trouble. I *told*

you you'd regret picking him over me," Micah said in frustrated anger.

That had been the extent of his fight to keep her. Telling her that she'd regret her choice. He'd felt that if he had to convince Johanna to stay with him, then he'd already lost her, and it hadn't been worth his breath to argue with her.

Taking out his worn, creased wallet, the one that carried his current ID stamped with his current name—one of many he'd assumed since he'd left Johanna and Cold Plains behind—he opened it. Beneath the handful of bills he always kept in it and the false ID was a tiny close-up of a sweet-faced girl with pale brown eyes and long, straight black hair.

Johanna's high school picture.

The same picture that was embossed in his brain. He couldn't say that it was embossed on his heart because he no longer had one. One of the hazards of his job. A heart only got in the way, slowed a man down, kept him from a laser-like focus on his assignment.

A wave of fury flared through his veins, and Micah crumpled the faded photo in his hand. He drew back his arm, about to pitch the tiny paper ball across the room, then changed his mind.

Exhaling a long, slow breath, he opened his hand, letting the small wad fall onto the bed. He carefully flattened it out again, then slipped the now-creased photograph back into his wallet.

Samuel couldn't be allowed to get away with this, Micah swore vehemently. He didn't know any of the particulars, but Samuel had to be behind Johanna's death. His twin brother's prints were all over this. He'd bet his soul on it.

The corners of Micah's mouth curved in a humorless smile.

If he had a soul, he corrected silently.

Micah knew someone who could look into things. Someone who could take Samuel's so-called paradise, strip it of all its gingerbread facade and expose it for what it was: hell on earth. Someone who he'd known all those years ago and had himself left for greener pastures, so to speak.

Someone, Micah thought as he tapped the numbers lodged in his memory out onto the cell phone's key pad, who still had a soul. And who knew, maybe even a heart, too.

The cell phone on the other end rang a total of six times. Micah decided to give it to the count of ten and then try again later.

A man in his profession didn't leave messages.

But then he heard someone picking up on the other end and a deep voice say, "Special Agent Bledsoe."

A glimmer of a smile passed over Micah's lips.

His brother was going down. It might take a while, but he was going down. And he would pay for what had happened to Johanna.

"Hawk, this is Micah. Grayson," he added in case the agent was having trouble remembering him. It had been a while. "I need to see you." He paused and then said cryptically, "I've got a not-so-anonymous tip for you about those murdered women on the news."

Chapter 1

Okay, so where is he?

Special Agent Hawk Bledsoe paced about the hotel room, which grew progressively smaller by the moment. His frown deepened significantly as impatience drummed through him.

He had a really bad feeling about this.

About *all* of this.

To say that he had been surprised to hear from Micah Grayson out of the blue yesterday after so many years gave new meaning to the term "understatement." Micah and he both had the very same connection between them that had just recently come to light about the five murder victims: they came from the same region in Wyoming. Micah was born in Horn's Gulf, while he had the misfortune of actually growing up in Cold Plains.

A great place to be from, Hawk thought cynically,

the heels of his boots sinking into the light gray carpet. He made yet another complete trip around the room. *Nothing good had ever come from that town. Except for—*

No! He wasn't going to let himself go there. Those thoughts belonged in his past, buried deeper than the unearthed five victims apparently had been.

The victims, he'd already decided after reviewing the notes made by past agents, had all been buried as if the killer had expected them to be discovered. Eventually, if not immediately.

Why? What was the sense in that? What did these women have in common other than having the bad luck of being from Cold Plains? And of course, other than the fact that they had all been murdered, execution style, with a single bullet to the back of the head. Their sins—whatever they were—had obviously been unpardonable to someone.

But who?

And why?

And where the hell was Micah, anyway? He was supposed to be here. The urgency in Micah's voice was the reason why he'd driven straight through the night to get here.

It wasn't as if he'd called the man—a man who he knew through various sources made his living by hiring out to do things that others either could not or would not do—or were just unable to do. Be that as it may, it was Micah who had called *him,* not the other way around.

Called him and had said just enough to get him hooked. That he needed to talk to him about the five murdered women who had been found scattered through isolated areas in Wyoming.

Did that mean Micah knew who was responsible? Or that he at least had a viable theory? He wished he could have gotten Micah to say more, but the man had been deliberately closemouthed, saying he'd tell him "everything" when he got here.

So where was he?

Hawk knew that Micah Grayson had once dated Johanna Tate. Was *that* why the man had gone out of his way to call him? Had he called in reinforcements? As far as he knew, that wasn't Micah's style.

Either way, it looked as if he wasn't about to find out now. He'd gotten no more out of his one-time friend than that: to come meet him in this off-the-beaten-path hotel. Room 705. Micah didn't believe in saying much over the phone, even one that most likely was one of those disposable models, which could be discarded— and rendered untraceable—at a moment's notice.

So rather than clear anything up, Micah's call had merely added to the mystery that was already so tightly wound around the dead women it reminded Hawk of a skein of yarn whose beginning was so well hidden, it defied discovery—or unraveling.

Yarn.

Where the *hell* had that come from?

And then he remembered.

She had liked to knit. He'd teased her about it, saying things like it was an old-lady hobby. Carly, in turn, had sniffed dismissively and informed him that it suited her just fine, thank you very much. He recalled being fascinated, watching her fingers manage the needles like a master, creating articles of clothing out of straight lines of color.

As he recalled, she had professed to absolutely *love* creating things.

Again, he banished the thoughts—the all-too-vivid memories—out of his head. But not quite as forcefully this time as he had initially. Hawk supposed that it was inevitable. After all this time, he was about to be dragged back to the little pimple of a town he'd once left behind in his rearview mirror.

He recalled driving away as fast as he could all those years ago. At the time, he'd thought he was leaving permanently. Obviously not.

He was making too much out of this. The thoughts he was having about Carly just went to prove that he was human, just like everyone else. Nothing more.

The problem was, he didn't want to be human. Especially not now of all times. If nothing else, being human, reacting emotionally, got in the way of efficiency. Being human was a distraction, and he had a case to unravel and a murderer—or murderers—to track down. That had to come first. He couldn't afford to be distracted, not even a little.

Memories and thoughts of what could have been—and *hadn't* been—had no place here. Or anywhere in his life.

Though his expression gave no evidence of his emotional turmoil, Hawk was too tense to sit down. So he went on pacing about the small hotel room where Micah had said he would meet him.

He'd been waiting for over an hour.

To the best of his recollection, Micah was *never* late. It was one of the things they'd had in common. Because of the directions that life had taken them, they both believed that time was a tool to be used, not frivolously ignored or disregarded.

Micah *wouldn't* be late. If the mercenary wasn't here it was because he *couldn't* be here.

Which meant that something was wrong.

Which in turn meant that he, as the special agent who had recently been put in charge of this case, couldn't put off the inevitable for very much longer.

The only thing that Micah had confirmed over the phone was what he'd already just learned: that all the victims were women from Cold Plains. In order to conduct the investigation properly, he would have to go up to Cold Plains, Wyoming, himself.

Looks like the prodigal son is coming home, he thought wryly.

Except that, in this case, he hadn't been prodigal so much as smart. Leaving Cold Plains had been the smartest thing he'd ever done. By the same token, returning might turn out to be the stupidest.

Hawk looked at his watch again. When he'd gotten here—and found the room empty—he'd mentally promised himself to give Micah approximately ninety minutes to show up. But right now, he was feeling way too antsy to wait for sixty more minutes to slip beyond his reach.

With a sigh, he crossed back to the hotel room door that had been deliberately left unlocked for him.

Damn it, Micah, I hope you haven't gotten yourself killed, he thought irritably. Because he was fairly certain that nothing short of death would have kept Micah Grayson from keeping an appointment that he himself had set up.

He needed to see the county coroner before he made his way to Cold Plains, but a visit to Cold Plains was definitely in his immediate future.

Biting off a curse, Hawk let himself out of the room and closed the door behind him.

It seemed rather incredible to Carly Finn that the two times she made up her mind to finally, *finally* leave Cold Plains, something came up to stop her.

And not some mild, inconsequential "something" but a major, pull-out-all-the-stops "something."

The first time she'd been ready to test her wings and fly, leaving this soul-draining speck of a town behind her and eagerly begin a fresh, new chapter of her life with the man she knew deep down in her soul she was meant to be with, her infinite sense of obligation as well as her never-ending sense of responsibility to her family had added lead to her wings and grounded her with a bone-jarring thud.

The problem then was that her father had been a drunk, a dyed-in-the-wool, leave-no-drink-untouched, hopeless alcoholic, and while there were many men— and women—with that shortcoming who could be considered by the rest of the world to be functioning alcoholics, her father hadn't fallen into that category. He hadn't been even close to a functioning alcoholic, and she knew that if she left with Hawk, if she accompanied the man she loved so much that it hurt so he could follow his dreams, she would be abandoning not just her father but her baby sister to a very cruel, inevitable life of poverty and, eventually, to homelessness. The baby sister she had promised her dying mother to look after all those years ago.

So she knew that in all good conscience, she had to remain. And remain she did. She remained in order to run the family farm and somehow juggle a job as a waitress, as well, the latter she undertook in order to bring in some extra, much-needed money into the household.

She remained while sending Hawk Bledsoe on his way with a lie ringing in his ears.

There was no other choice. She knew that the only way she could get Hawk to leave Cold Plains—and her—so that he could follow his dreams was to tell him that she didn't love him anymore. That she had actually *never* loved him and had decided that she just couldn't go on pretending anymore.

Because she knew that if she didn't, if she let him know how much she really loved him, Hawk would stay in Cold Plains with her. He would marry her, and eventually, he would become very bitter as he entertained thoughts of what "could have been but wasn't."

She couldn't do that to him. Couldn't allow him to do that to himself.

Loving someone meant making sacrifices. So she'd made the ultimate sacrifice: she'd lied to him and sent him on his way, while she had stayed behind to do what she had to do. And struggled not to die by inches with each passing day.

But the day finally came when she had had enough. When she had silently declared her independence, not just from the farm but from the town, which had become downright frightening in a short period. Cold Plains had gone from a dead-end town to a sleek, picture-perfect one that had sold its soul to the devil.

She'd reached the conclusion that she had a right to live her own life. That went for Mia, the baby sister she had always doted on, as well.

She didn't even want to pack, content to leave everything behind just so that she and Mia could get a brand-new start. But she was in for a startling surprise. Somehow, while she was doing all that juggling to keep the farm—and them—afloat, Mia had grown up and formed opinions of her own—or rather, as it turned out, had them formed for her.

When she had told Mia that the day had finally come, that she'd had enough and that they were leaving Cold Plains for good, her beautiful, talented baby sister had knocked her for a loop by telling her flatly that she was staying.

It got worse.

Mia was not just staying, but she was "planning" on marrying Brice Carrington, a wealthy widower more than twice her age.

"But you don't love him," Carly had protested when she had finally recovered from the shock.

The expression on Mia's face had turned nasty. "Yes, I do," her sister had insisted. "Besides, how would you know if I did or didn't? You're always so busy working, you don't have time to notice anything. You certainly don't have any time for me. Not like Samuel does," she'd added proudly, with the air of one who had been singled out and smiled down upon by some higher power.

The accusation had stung, especially since the only reason she had been working so hard was to provide for Mia in the first place. But the sudden realization that while she'd been busy trying to make a life for them, trying to save money so that they could finally get away from here, her sister had been brainwashed.

There was no other term for it. What Samuel Grayson did, with his silver tongue, his charm and his exceedingly handsome face was pull people into his growing circle of followers. Pull them in and mesmerize them with rhetoric. Make them believe that whatever he suggested they do was really their idea in the first place.

Why else would Mia believe that she was actually in love with a man who was old enough to be her father. Older. Brice Carrington was as bland as a bowl of unsalted, white rice. He was also, in the hierarchy of things, currently very high up in Samuel Grayson's social structure.

Maybe Brice represented the father they'd never really had, Carly guessed. Or maybe, since their dad was dead, Mia was looking for someone to serve as a substitute?

In any case, if Mia was supposed to marry Brice Carrington, it was because the match suited Grayson's grand plan.

The very thought of Grayson made her angry. But at the moment, it was an anger that had no suitable outlet. She couldn't just go railing against the man as if she was some kind of a lunatic. For one thing, most of the people who still lived in town thought Samuel Grayson was nothing short of the Second Coming.

Somehow, in the past five years, while no one was paying attention, Samuel Grayson and a few of his handpicked associates had managed to buy up all the property in Cold Plains. At first, moving stealthily but always steadily, he'd wound up arranging everything up to and possibly including the rising and setting of the sun to suit his own specifications and purposes.

These days, it seemed as if nothing took place in Cold Plains without his say-so or close scrutiny. He had eyes and ears everywhere. Anyone who opposed him was either asked to leave or, and this seemed to be more and more the case, they just disappeared.

At first glance, it appeared as if the man had done a great deal for the town. Old buildings had been renovated, and new buildings had gone up, as well. There was now a new town hall, a brand-new school, which he oversaw and for which he only hired teachers who were devoted to his ideology. And most important of all, he'd built a bright, spanking, brand-new church, one he professed was concerned strictly with the well-being of its parishioners' souls—and that, he had not been shy about saying, was the purview of the leader of the flock: Grayson himself.

To a stranger from the outside, it looked like a pretty little, idyllic town.

To her, Cold Plains had become a town filled with puppets—and Samuel Grayson was the smiling, grand puppeteer. A puppeteer whose every dictate was slavishly followed. His call for modesty had all the women who belonged to his sect wearing dresses that would have been more at home on the bodies of performers reenacting the late 1950s.

Maybe her skepticism was because she'd grown up listening to her late father's promises, none of which he'd ever kept. Promises that, for the most part, he didn't even recall making once a little time had gone by.

Whatever the reason, she didn't trust Samuel Grayson any further than she could throw him. And he was a large, powerful-looking man.

Her sense of survival was urgently prompting her to leave before something went wrong—before she *couldn't* leave.

But no matter what she felt about Cold Plains's transformation and no matter what her sense of survival dictated, she was not about to leave town without her sister. And Mia had flatly refused to budge, declaring instead her intentions of staying.

She was, Carly caught herself thinking again, between the proverbial rock and hard place.

Common sense might prod her to make a run for it, but she had never put her own well-being above someone else's, especially that of a loved one.

That was why she'd lied to Hawk to make him leave Cold Plains and why she was still here now, doing her best to pretend to be one of Samuel's most recent converts even though the very thought made her sick to her stomach.

In her opinion, Samuel Grayson, once merely a very slick motivational speaker, was now orchestrating a utopian-like environment where allegiance to him was the prime directive and where, by instituting a society of blindly obedient, non-thinking robots, he was setting the cause of civilization back over fifty years.

Women in Samuel's society were nothing more than subservient, second-class citizens whose main function, Carly strongly suspected, was to bear children and populate Grayson's new world.

She'd heard, although hadn't quite managed to confirm, that Samuel was even having these devoted women "branded." Horrified, she'd looked into it and discovered that they were being tattooed with the small letter *D,* for devotee, on their right hips. That alone made the man a crazed megalomaniac.

Although it sickened her, Carly knew she had to play up to Samuel in order to get her sister to trust her enough so that she could eventually abduct her and get her away from this awful place. Nothing short of that was going to work—and even that might not—but she had no other options open to her.

Hoping that Samuel would eventually grow tired of his little game—or that someone would get sick of his playing the not-so-benevolent dictator—and send him on his way was akin to waiting for Godot. It just wasn't going to happen.

So she'd gone to Samuel and insisted that she was qualified to fill the teaching position that had suddenly opened up at the Cold Plains Day Care Center. A smile that she could only describe as reptilian had spread over Samuel's handsome, tanned face. Steepling his long, aristocratic fingers together, he fixed his gaze intently on her face.

He paused dramatically for effect as the moment sank in, then said, "Yes, my dear, I am sure that you are more than qualified to fill that position, and may I say how very happy I am that you have come around and decided to come join us." He'd taken her hand between his and though his smile had never wavered, it had sent chills through her. Chills she wasn't quite sure how to dodge. She'd never felt more of a sense of imprisonment than she had at that moment.

"You will be a most welcomed addition," he had assured her.

She remembered thinking, *Over my dead body*, and she had meant it.

The problem was she was fairly certain that the coda, although silently said, would not be a deterrent to Grayson. He was a man who allowed nothing to stand in the way of his plans. To that end, he was perfectly capable of cutting out a person's heart without missing a beat.

She *had* to get Mia away from here. And she would, even if it wound up being the last thing she ever did.

Chapter 2

"Hi, Doc. This is going to have to be quick. I've only got a few minutes to spare," Hawk said by way of a greeting as he walked into the county coroner's office.

In reality, since Micah hadn't shown up for their appointed meeting, he should have skipped coming here altogether and gone on straight to Cold Plains. But the coroner had called, saying there was something that he needed to tell him. And if he was being honest and had his choice in the matter, he would have gladly stalled and remained here indefinitely, at this temporary FBI outpost. But he didn't have a choice, and he could only spare a few minutes.

At this point, he would have welcomed being sidetracked by anything, and this included an earthquake, a tornado or a tsunami, none of which ever occurred in this rough-and-tumble region of Wyoming. But although he would rather do *anything* than go on to Cold Plains to investigate exactly how these five murdered women were connected, Hawk was first and foremost a dedicated FBI agent, and he wasn't about to let any of his past personal feelings get in the way of his trying to solve this case.

Not bothering to shrug out of his jacket, Hawk crossed over to the coroner. He'd only met the man a few days before but the coroner took his job very seriously.

"Why did you call me?" Hawk asked. "Did you find out anything new?"

"Not exactly," Dr. Hermann Keegan replied, measuring his words out slowly, as if he wanted to be sure they were absolutely right before he uttered them. He looked at Hawk over the tops of his rimless reading glasses. "Actually, what I found was something old."

His mind on the ordeal that lay ahead of him, Hawk had very little patience with what sounded like a riddle. "Come again?"

"Once the fact that they were all connected came to light, I pulled the autopsy records of the other four victims," he explained. "Were you aware of the fact that the 'tattoo' the deputy coroner found on victim number two's right hip washed off when he was cleaning the body?"

Victim number two was the only female they hadn't been able to identify yet. All the others had names, but this one was still referred to as Jane Doe four years after she'd been discovered. The woman's DNA and fingerprints turned out not to be a match for anyone currently in any of the FBI databases.

"Tattoos don't wash off," Hawk pointed out.

Doc Keegan smiled, making his spherical, moonlike face appear even rounder. "Exactly. According to the notes, the letter, a *d,* appeared to have been drawn in with some kind of permanent, black laundry marker or maybe a Sharpie." He raised his eyes to Hawk's. "You know what that means, don't you?"

"Yeah," Hawk answered crisply. "Either this woman had a penchant for marking up her body—or she wasn't really one of the cult's followers but was pretending to be for some reason." Being a law enforcement agent, the first thing that struck him was that Jane Doe might have been one, as well. "She might have been under-cover," he concluded.

Keegan's head bobbed up and down. "My money's on that."

Hawk looked at the five manila folders that were fanned out on top of the coroner's extremely cluttered desk. Each was labeled with the name of a different victim. Besides Jane Doe, there was Shelby Jackson who had been found first in Gulley, Wyoming, five years ago, Laurel Pierce, found in Cheyenne three years ago, Abby Michaels, discovered in the woods outside of Laramie last year and Johanna Tate, found in Eden last week.

Johanna Tate.

Micah's former girlfriend, Hawk suddenly remembered. The name had been nagging at him ever since he'd heard the news. Was that why Micah had called him? Because of Johanna?

Did Micah know more than he'd alluded to? Had he decided to take matters into his own hands? Going outside the law had become a way of life for him, and he would have thought nothing of avenging Johanna's murder. Had it backfired on him because he'd let his emotions get in the way?

Damn it, he needed answers, Hawk thought, frustrated. Nodding toward the folders, he asked, "Mind if I take those with me?"

Stepping away from Joanna Tate's lifeless body he'd finished sewing together, Keegan scrubbed and then pushed the files together into one pile. "Be my guest," he told Hawk. "I've already made copies of them for you."

Hawk scooped up the files. Already familiar with all the victims, he wanted to review the files in depth and was grateful to the coroner for making copies for him. Still stumped, he needed all the input he could get his hands on.

"You're pretty thorough," Hawk commented.

Keegan raised his slopping shoulders and let them fall again. "I've got the time to be. This is the most amount of action this office has seen in a very long while."

"What do you do the rest of the time?" Hawk asked, curious what occupied the man's time when he wasn't conducting an autopsy. He sincerely doubted that Wyoming was a hotbed of homicides.

Keegan's answer surprised him.

"I'm a vet," the older man replied. "Technically," he explained as a look of disbelief came over the special agent's face, "I don't even have to be a doctor of any kind in order to become a coroner. I just have to be unusually observant and display a high tolerance when it comes to the dissection of dead bodies. Like this one." He nodded at the draped body on his steel table.

"Good to know," Hawk quipped. Holding the files to his chest, he crossed to the door. "Thanks again for these."

"My pleasure," Keegan answered, adding, "so to speak."

Closing the door behind him, Hawk blew out a breath. "Yeah," he muttered to himself in a low voice. "So to speak," he echoed.

He squared his shoulders and made his way out of the building and back to his car. He was all out of excuses and reasons to delay his departure. He'd already gotten in contact with his team and told them to temporarily set up a "satellite FBI office" in a cabin several miles out of town.

They were probably already there, he thought. Now it was his turn. Hawk turned his key in the ignition and listened to his car come to life.

Next up: Cold Plains.

Ready or not, here I come.

Carly was standing outside the school where she had so recently taken a position, supervising the children as they made the most of their afternoon recess.

That was where she was when she first saw him. First saw the ghost from her past.

That was what she initially thought she was seeing, a ghost, a figment of her wandering imagination. A momentary hallucination on her part, brought on by a combination of stress and anger and the overwhelming need to have someone to lean on—just for a little while.

For her, the only one she had ever had to lean on had been Hawk, but that had been a very long time ago. At least ten years in her past, she judged.

Maybe even more.

The bottom line was that there was absolutely no reason for her to see Hawk Bledsoe getting out of a relatively new, black sedan. The vehicle had just pulled up before the pristine edifice which housed The Grayson Community Center as well as the living quarters of several of Samuel Grayson's top people.

Or, as she was wont to think of them in the privacy of her own mind, Grayson's henchmen.

Her mind was playing tricks on her, Carly silently insisted. Any second now, this person she had conjured up would fade away or take on the features of someone else, someone who she knew from town. Someone she was accustomed to seeing day in, day out.

She waited, not daring to breathe.

He wasn't fading. Wasn't changing.

Suddenly feeling very light-headed, Carly sucked a huge breath into her lungs.

Ordinarily, fresh air helped clear her head. But it wasn't her head that needed clearing, it was her eyes, because she was still seeing him.

Or at least a version of him.

The boyish look she'd known—and loved—was gone, replaced by a face that, aside from being incredibly handsome, was thinner and far more somber looking. Otherwise, it was still him, still Hawk. He was still tall, still muscular—the navy windbreaker he wore did nothing to hide that fact. And he still had sandy-blond hair, even though it was cut shorter now than it had been the last time she had laid eyes on him.

And when he made eye contact with her from across the street, she saw that the apparition with Hawk's face had the same deep, warm, brown eyes that Hawk had had.

Eyes that could melt her soul.

She felt her pulse accelerating, her heart hammering as if it was recreating a refrain from The Anvil Chorus in double time.

Why wasn't this image, this apparition, this ghost from the depths of her mind fading? Why was it coming toward her?

Carly's breath caught in her throat, all but solidifying and threatening to choke her. Even so, for the life of her, Carly just couldn't make herself look away.

She was still waiting for the image to break up—or for the world to end, whichever was more doable—as the distance between them continued to lessen.

When Hawk had first driven slowly through the town, heading for its center, its "heart," Hawk had to admit that he was rather stunned. The town appeared to have gone through an incredible amount of changes.

When he had left, Cold Plains looked to be on the verge of simply drying up and blowing away, a dying town abandoned by all but the very hopeless. Those who were devoid of ambition and who couldn't make a go of it anywhere else had chosen to remain here and die along with the town.

There was no sign of that town here.

This was more of a town that could take center stage in a children's storybook. All around him, there were new buildings. The ones that looked remotely familiar had all been restored, revitalized, given not just a new coat of paint but a new purpose.

The streets were repaired and clean. Actually clean, he marveled, remembering how filthy everything had appeared to be when he was growing up here.

The smell of fertilizer was missing, he suddenly realized. Cold Plains now seemed like a town on its way to becoming a city rather than a hovel disintegrating into a ghost town.

For a moment he thought that he was in the wrong place, that he had somehow gotten turned around while coming here and had managed to drive to another town. A brighter, newer town.

But then he saw a few faces he recognized, people he'd known growing up. That told him that this *was* Cold Plains. At the same time, he began to take note of not just the newly constructed buildings but the people, as well. Briskly moving people. People who seemed to have a purpose.

He saw several parents holding on to their children's hands, heading for what appeared to be a playground.

He did a mental double take. A playground? Since when was that part of the landscape? Or an ice cream parlor, for that matter?

"Excuse me, young man, didn't mean to almost walk into you." An older man laughed, sidestepping around him at the last moment. Hawk couldn't help staring at the white-haired man. He wore color-coordinated sweats, fancy, high-end sneakers—running shoes?— and he was holding navy-blue-colored weights in his hand that looked to be about a pound each.

He was power walking, Hawk realized.

Had everyone lost their minds?

He looked around again. All the people who were out and about appeared to be smiling. *Every last one of them.* It was almost eerie. And then he looked closer at the women who were passing him. Smiling, as well, they were all modestly dressed. No jeans, no scruffy cutoffs or overalls. Each and every one of them, young or old, children or adults, they were all wearing dresses.

Dresses that came down past the middle of their calves.

Hell, they all looked like extras from a movie about Amish life, Hawk thought. All that was missing were those hats or bonnets or whatever those things that all but hid their hair were called—

Hawk froze.

A second ago, he'd been busy scanning the immediate area, trying to reconcile what he was seeing with the Cold Plains citizens he remembered from his past. Lost in thought, he'd forgotten to get himself prepared, and so he wasn't.

Wasn't prepared to have the sight of her, wearing one of those ridiculous, sexless dresses, slam into him like a runaway freight train sliding down a steep embankment. Plowing straight into his gut.

He had to concentrate in order to draw in half a breath.

Carly.

Carly Finn.

The woman who had led him on, then skewered his insides and left him without so much as a backward glance. Left him to live or die, no matter to her.

Why the hell hadn't he realized that she would probably still be here? Still be living on the outskirts of Cold Plains?

This was where that stupid farm was, the one that meant so much more to her than he did, so of course she was still going to be here.

Still here and, despite the unbecoming, shapeless brown sack she wore, still as beautiful as she'd ever been.

More, he amended.

Even at this distance, he could see that Carly, with her long, blond hair pulled back into a ponytail, was even more beautiful than he remembered. Maybe that was because he'd been trying so hard to bury her image, to scrape it from his mind.

His hands were clenched at his sides. Fury raged through him, but there was no outlet. He couldn't afford to allow himself one.

Damn it, he wished he could just walk away. This minute. Wished he could get into his car and just drive until he ran out of gas or purged her image from his mind, whichever happened first.

But he couldn't, and he knew it, so there was no sense in wishing. He owed it to the Bureau to see this through, and he owed it to those five dead women to find their killer or killers. He wasn't a kid anymore who could just think of himself. He had responsibilities, even if he no longer possessed a viable heart.

Incensed, stunned, angry and a whole vanguard of other emotions he couldn't even begin to catalog yet, Hawk found himself striding straight for the woman clad in the unflattering brown dress.

When she saw him heading for her, Carly's very first reaction was to want to bolt and run.

But she didn't.

She had never run away from anything in her life and she was not about to start now—no matter how much she wanted to and how much easier it would have been than to wait for him to reach her.

Leaning for support against the white picket fence, which ran along the length of the school yard, Carly raised her chin, said a silent prayer that she *wasn't* losing her mind and waited for the approaching man to turn into someone else.

He didn't.

So much for the power of positive thinking.

Her thoughts did a complete one-eighty. Okay, so it *was* Hawk. What was he doing here? Of all the times she'd yearned for him to return, this was the worst possible one.

She couldn't allow herself to forget what she was still

doing here. She had to remember why she'd taken this job at the day care center and why she forced herself to smile at Samuel Grayson when she would rather just drive a stake through his heart, grab her sister's hand and run.

"Carly?"

The second she heard his voice, a wave of heat, then cold, then heat again washed over her. For the tiniest split second, the world shrank down to a pinprick. Only sheer willpower on her part caused it to widen again, chasing away the blackness that threatened to swallow her up whole.

Taking another deep, calming breath, she responded, "Yes?"

"Carly," Hawk repeated, his voice more somber this time, more forceful. His dark brown eyes all but bore into her. "It's Hawk."

She hadn't wanted to run her tongue along her lips in order to moisten them, but if she didn't, she wouldn't have been able to utter another sound.

"Yes," she answered quietly, praying he wouldn't hear her heart pounding. "I know."

A sixth sense she'd developed these past five years warned her that she was being observed. Observed by someone whose loyalty was strictly to Samuel and who in all likelihood reported everything he saw directly to the man. She had to be careful. Everything was riding on making Samuel believe that she, like all the other women in the sect, was under his spell as well as firmly under his thumb. It went against everything she was, everything she had ever stood for, but to save Mia, she was willing to play this part.

That meant that she had to seem almost indifferent to the man she'd once loved above all else.

A man she still loved.

Carly swallowed as unobtrusively as she could and then forced a bright, mindless smile to her lips as she asked cheerfully, "So what brings you back to Cold Plains after all this time?"

Chapter 3

It *looked* like Carly. Even in that ridiculous, shapeless sack of a dress, it still looked like a slightly older, but definitely a heart-stoppingly beautiful version of Carly.

But it didn't *sound* like Carly.

Oh, it was her voice all right. He would have recognized her voice anywhere, under any circumstances. There were times he still heard her voice in his dreams, dreams that had their roots in a different, far less complicated time. And then, when he'd wake up in the dark and alone, he would upbraid himself for being so weak as to yearn for her. An emptiness would come over him, hollowing out what had once been his heart.

Yes, it was her voice all right. But there was a decided lack of *spirit* evident in it, a lack of the feisty, independent essence that made Carly who she was. That made her Carly.

The bright, chipper, vapid question she'd just asked sounded as if it had come from a Carly who had been lobotomized.

Which was, he now realized, exactly the way he could have described the expressions on the faces of several of the men and women he'd just watched walk by. It really looked to him as if nothing was behind the smiles on their faces. Granted they were moving about with what appeared to be a sense of purpose, but they all came across as being only two-dimensional—as if they had been cut out of cardboard and mounted on sticks.

Damn it, talk, *Hawk,* Carly thought. *Say something so I can go on with this charade. You will never,* never *know how much I've missed you, how many times I'd lie awake, wondering where you were and what you were doing. Wondering if you missed me even just a little.*

Carly had never allowed herself to regret sending him away. It had been the right thing to do. The right thing for *him.* But oh, how she regretted not being with Hawk when he had left town.

And now he was here, standing before her, larger than life—and she couldn't tell him anything. Not how she felt, not why she was going through the motions of being one of Samuel Grayson's devoted followers.

"So?" Carly prodded, still keeping the same wide, vacant smile on her lips. Her facial muscles began to cramp up. Playing mindless was a lot harder than it looked. "What brings you back?" she asked him again.

Carly knew it couldn't be a family matter that had caused him to return. His mother was dead—she had been the only thing keeping him here in the first place—and he never got along with his father who, although kinder in spirit than hers, had the very same romance going with any bottle of liquor he could find, just as her late father had had.

"You're about the very last person I would have ever expected to see coming back to Cold Plains." That much, at least, was truthful.

He laughed shortly as he shook his head. The sound had no humor in it. "Funny, and I figured you had enough sense to leave here," he replied, his tone sounding edgier than he'd meant it to.

Carly shrugged, momentarily looking away. But the children were all playing nicely. No squabbles that needed refereeing on her part. She had no excuse to leave.

She tried to tell herself that Hawk's words didn't sting, but it was a lie. Even after all this time, his opinion still meant a great deal to her. It probably always would.

"Something came up," she said by way of an excuse—and, again, she was being truthful. Something *had* come up to keep her here. Her sister's marriage bombshell.

Hawk's eyes skimmed over the dress she wore. He tried to do his best not to imagine the slender, firm body beneath the fabric or to remember that one night that she had been his. He hadn't realized then that he was merely on borrowed time.

"Yeah," he said curtly. "I can see that."

She sincerely doubted that he hated the dress she had on as much as she did, but wearing it was necessary. It was all part of convincing that hideous megalomaniac that she was as brainwashed as everyone else who had joined his so-called "flock."

"You still haven't answered my question," Carly prodded gently, her curiosity mounting. "Why are you back in Cold Plains?"

He minced no words. The days when he had wanted to shield her were gone. "I'm trying to find out who killed five young women and left their bodies to rot in five different, remote locations in Wyoming."

She looked at him sharply. Had he struck a chord? Did she actually know something about these women who had been cut down so ruthlessly? But then the look vanished, and her expression became completely un-readable. He swore inwardly.

The next moment, a strange smile curved her lips. "So you did it," she concluded, nodding her head with approval.

Hawk narrowed his eyes in annoyed confusion. "Did what?"

He'd told her that he wanted to do something adven-turous, something that mattered. He wanted to leave the world a better place than when he found it. It was why she'd made him leave. Someone like that couldn't be happy in a town the size of a shoe box.

"You became a law enforcement agent. A U.S. Mar-shal?" she asked, guessing which branch he had ulti-mately joined. It had to be something along those lines in order to give him the authority and jurisdiction to investigate a crime like the one he had just mentioned.

Hawk shook his head. Then because she was obviously waiting for a clarification, he said, "I'm with the FBI."

"Even more impressive."

Working for the FBI wasn't impressive as far as he was concerned. It was a job, something that allowed him to move about, to keep from being tempted to put down roots in any one place for long. And it allowed him to keep the rest of the world at bay. For that, he had her to thank. After she had broken his heart, telling him that she had never loved him, he'd decided that he would never subject himself to that kind of pain again. The only way to do that was not to allow anyone in. Not to form any attachments.

Ever.

So what was he doing, standing here, feeling as if he'd just walked through a portal and gone back in time again? What the hell was he doing *feeling* again? It seemed that no matter what his resolve, all it took to undo everything he'd built up in the last decade or so was to be in Carly's presence again for a few minutes.

It just didn't seem right, but there it was, anyway.

"It's a job," he told her, shrugging off her compliment.

She heard the indifference, the callousness, even if he wasn't aware of expressing them. A wave of concern came over her. Maybe she shouldn't have turned him away. Not if it had turned out all wrong.

"Then you're disappointed?" she asked.

The thought that he was disillusioned sliced away at her heart. She had made what to her was the ultimate sacrifice, sending Hawk away so that he could follow his dream. If his dream had turned out not to be what he really wanted, then all these lost years had been for nothing.

"Yes," he answered coldly as his eyes skimmed over her again.

He wasn't talking about his job, she realized. Hawk was talking about how he felt about her. More than anything in the world, she would have loved to have set him straight, to tell him what she was really still doing here, but if she did that, she would wind up instantly throwing away everything she'd done up until now. It would mean sacrificing all the work she'd put into making Samuel believe that she was one of the faithful. One of the "devotees" he took such relish in collecting and adding to his number.

"Why are you dressed like that?" Hawk demanded, frowning. He looked around as he asked the question, adding, "Why are all the women out here dressed like that?"

"Not all," Carly pointed out, doing her best not to let her relief over that little fact show through. "There are still holdouts."

Thank God, she added silently.

"'Holdouts,'" he echoed her words. "As in, not having found the 'right path'?"

She widened the forced smile on her lips, hating this charade that circumstances had forced her to play. "I see you do understand."

He felt contempt. Had she always been this weak and he hadn't noticed, blinded by the so-called sacrifices she'd made to keep her father's farm running?

"Not by a long shot," he answered, disgusted. Again, he looked around. From all indications, they were standing in the center of town. And yet, it was all wrong, conflicting with his memories. The town he had left behind had been a rough-and-tumble place, a place where people existed without the promise of a future. A place where grizzled, weathered men came in to wash the taste of stagnation and failure from their parched throats at the local bar.

The bar was conspicuously missing as were other establishments that he remembered having once occupied the streets of Cold Plains.

"Where's the hardware store?" he asked. There was a health club—a damn health club of all things!—standing where he could have *sworn* the hardware store had once been.

Since when did the people who lived here have time to idle away, lifting weights and sitting in saunas? Health clubs were for the pampered with time on their hands. Nobody he knew in Cold Plains was like that. They had livings to scratch out from an unforgiving earth.

Or, at least, nobody had *been* like that when he'd left all those years ago.

Obviously things had changed.

"The owner had to relocate to Bryson," she told him, mentioning the name of a neighboring town. "He couldn't afford the rent here anymore." She saw confusion in Hawk's sharp eyes as he cocked his head. It took everything she had not to raise her hand and run her fingers along his cheek, the way she used to when he would look at her like that.

With effort, she blocked the memory. "New people came in and started buying up the land—investing in Cold Plains," she explained, quoting the official story that had been given out about the changes. Changes, everyone had been told over and over, that were all "for the better."

"And the diner?" Hawk asked, nodding toward a place down the block. The diner was clearly gone, replaced by another, far more modern-looking restaurant with a pretentious name. "Exactly what the hell is a 'Vegetarian Café'?"

"Just what the name suggests it is," she replied, then added, "They serve much healthier food than the diner ever did."

The name indicated that no meat was served on the premises. From where he stood, that just didn't compute. "This is cattle country," Hawk protested. "Men like their steaks, their meat, not some funny-looking, wilted green things." As he spoke, it struck him that the people who continued to walk by him all seemed to have the same eerie, neat and tidy and completely-devoid-of-any-character appearance as the new buildings did. "Speaking of which, where the hell *are* all the men?" he asked.

She knew what he meant, but of necessity, she pretended to be confused by his question. "They're all around you," she answered, indicating the ones who were out with their families or just briskly walking from one destination to another.

"No, they're not," he bit off. He'd grown up here, had lived among them. The men who had lived in Cold Plains when he was a teenager spent their days wrestling with the elements, fighting the land as they struggled to make a living, to provide for their families and themselves. The men he saw now looked too soft for that. Too fake. "These guys look like they're all about to audition for a remake of *The Stepford Wives.*"

"Lower your voice," Carly said, using a more forceful tone than he'd heard coming from her up until now. *That* was the Carly he remembered, he thought.

But it bothered him that she was looking around, appearing concerned. As if she was afraid that someone would overhear them.

What the hell had happened to Cold Plains?

To her?

"Or what?" he challenged. "Whatever great power turned all these guys into drones will strike me dead for blaspheming?" he demanded angrily. "Who *did* all this?" he asked. "Who made everyone so damn fake?" But before Carly had a chance to answer him, Hawk shot another question at her. "You can't tell me that you actually *like* living this way, like some mindless preprogrammed robot."

Though his tone was angry, he was all but pleading with her to contradict his initial impression, to let him know somehow that she was here looking like some 1950s housewife against her will. That she didn't *want* to be like this.

Carly forced herself to spout the party line. "Samuel Grayson has generously done a great deal for this town," she began, the words all but burning a hole through her tongue.

"Grayson?" Hawk repeated. She was talking about Micah's twin brother. The smooth talker of the pair. He remembered thinking that the man could have easily been a snake oil salesman in the Old West. Last he'd heard, Grayson had hit the trail, spouting nonsense. They called that being a "motivational speaker" these days. Still a snake oil salesman in his book. "Samuel Grayson did all this?"

She nodded, forcing herself to look both enthusiastic and respectful at the mere mention of the man's name. "He and the investors he brought with him," she told him.

She hated the look of disbelief and disappointment she saw in Hawk's eyes, but she knew she couldn't risk telling him the way she actually felt. Couldn't tell him that she knew Grayson, charming though he might seem at first, was guilty of brainwashing the more gullible, the more desperate of the town's citizens. These were people who had tried to eke out a living for so long that when they had been given comforts for the very first time in their lives, they'd willingly fallen under the man's spell. They had given their allegiance to Grayson gladly, never realizing that they were also trading in their souls. Samuel Grayson accepted nothing less than complete submission. He fed on the power he had over the growing population of the so-called, little utopian world he had created.

So the rumors and his first impression were right, Hawk thought grimly. This was what Micah had vaguely alluded to when he'd asked to meet with him. Samuel Grayson had established a cult out here, preying on the vulnerable, the desperate, the easily swayed. He'd used all that against them to establish a beachhead for his particular brand of lunatic fringe.

"And where is Samuel Grayson right now?" he asked.

Again, the words all but scalded Carly's tongue, but she had no choice. She'd seen one of Samuel's henchmen come around the back of the school yard. The man didn't even bother pretending that he wasn't watching her. It was enough to make a person deeply paranoid.

"Samuel is wherever he is needed the most," she replied.

Without fully realizing what he was doing, Hawk took hold of her shoulders, fighting the very strong urge to shake her, return her to the clearheaded, intelligent woman he'd once known—or at least believed he'd once known.

Exasperation filled his veins as he cried, "Oh God, Carly, you can't possibly really believe what you just spouted."

Carly forced herself to raise her chin the way she always used to when she was bracing for a fight. "Of course I believe what I just said. And I'm not 'spouting,' I'm repeating the truth."

Hawk rolled his eyes, battling disgust.

"There a problem here?" someone asked directly behind him.

The low, gravelly voice belonged to the town's chief of police, one Bo Fargo. It was a job title that Fargo had apparently bestowed upon himself. The title elevated him from the lowly position of sheriff, a job he had just narrowly been elected to in the first place. But he did Grayson's bidding and, as such, was assured of a job for life, no matter what.

Carly's eyes widened.

"No, no problem," she declared quickly, hoping to avert this from turning into something ugly, given half a chance. She knew how Fargo operated. The stocky man didn't believe in just throwing his weight around but in using his fists and the butt of his gun to do his "convincing," as well. She didn't want to see Hawk hurt. "I'm just telling Hawk here about all the changes that have been introduced to Cold Plains—thanks to Samuel—since he left here."

The name obviously struck a chord. Fargo squinted as he peered up into Hawk's face.

In his fifties, the tall, husky man was accustomed to having both men and women alike cowering before him whenever he scowled. He enjoyed watching the spineless citizens being intimidated by him. He went so far as to relish it.

"Hawk?" Fargo echoed as he stared at the outsider through watery blue eyes.

"Hawk Bledsoe," Carly prompted by way of a reminder. "You remember Hawk, don't you, Chief?" she prodded, watching the man's round face for some sign of recognition.

"Tall, skinny kid," Fargo said, deliberately taking a derogatory tone.

Hawk gave no indication that he was about to back away. "I filled out some."

There was another moment of silence, as if Fargo was debating which way to play this. Hawk was not easily intimidated, and Fargo clearly didn't want to get into a contest where he might wind up being the loser. So for now, he laughed and patted his own gut.

"Haven't we all?" he asked rhetorically. "So what brings you back, Bledsoe? You thinking of resettling here in Cold Plains now that it's finally got something to offer?" he asked.

Hawk's eyes never left Fargo's. "No, I'm here to investigate the murders of five of your town's female citizens."

To back up his statement, Hawk took out his wallet and held up his ID for the chief to see.

If he didn't know better, Hawk thought, he would have sworn that Fargo turned pale beneath his deeply tanned face.

Chapter 4

The next minute, Hawk saw the chief of police pull himself together. What appeared to have been a momentary lapse, a chink in his armor, disappeared without a trace. Instead, a steely confidence descended over the older man's features again, eliminating any hint that he had been unnerved by talk of an investigation.

"I'm afraid that someone's been pulling your leg, Bledsoe," Fargo told him in a measured, firm voice. "We don't allow any crime here in Cold Plains."

Talk about being pompous, Hawk thought. The man set the bar at a new height. "Well, whether you allow it or not, Sheriff—"

"Chief," Fargo corrected tersely. "I'm the *chief* of police here."

Hawk inclined his head. If the man wanted to play games, so be it. He could play along for now, as long as it bought him some time and he could continue with his investigation. Not that he thought Fargo would be of any help to him. He just didn't want the man to be a hindrance.

"Chief," Hawk echoed, then continued, "but those five women are still dead nonetheless."

Minute traces of a scowl took over Fargo's average features. "I run a very tight ship here, Bledsoe. Everyone's happy, everyone gets along. Look around you," he instructed gruffly as he gestured about to encompass the entire town. "In case you haven't noticed, this isn't the town you left behind when you tore out of here after graduation." His eyes narrowed with the intention of pinning his opponent down. "I've been the chief of police these last five years and I don't recall anyone finding any bodies of dead women in Cold Plains," he concluded, closing the subject as far as he was concerned.

"That's because they weren't found here," Hawk explained evenly. "The bodies were discovered in five different locations throughout Wyoming over the last five years."

The expression on Fargo's face said that the matter was settled by the FBI agent's own admission. "Well, if you know that, then I don't understand what you're doing here, trying to stir things up. We're a peaceful little town, and we don't need your kind of trouble here."

A "peaceful little town" with a whole lot of secrets in its closet, Hawk was willing to bet. Out loud he said,

"All the women are believed to have been from here at one time or another."

"Hell, what someone does once they leave Cold Plains isn't any concern of mine." Though he continued to maintain the mirthless smile on his lips, Fargo's eyes seemed to bore into the man he considered an interloper—and possibly a problem. "If they found you dead, say in Cheyenne, that wouldn't be a reflection on the place where you were born, now, would it, Bledsoe?"

Hawk knew when he was being threatened and none-too-subtly at that. He had a feeling that Carly knew, too, because he saw her grow rigid, and just for a moment, that empty smile on her face had faded. She almost looked like the Carly he remembered, the Carly he still carried around in his head, despite all his efforts not to.

"It would be if I was killed here and then *moved* to Cheyenne," Hawk countered calmly.

He saw a flash of anger in the watery eyes before the chief got himself under control. "Is that what you're saying, Bledsoe? That these women were killed here and then somehow magically *lifted* and deposited in different places, all without my knowing a thing about it?" He drew closer, more menacing. "You think I'm that blind?"

"No, I don't," Hawk answered evenly. "And what I'm saying is that I need to investigate their deaths further, and that since they did come from Cold Plains, I wanted to ask a few questions starting here."

Fargo crossed his arms before him, an immovable

brick wall. *Daring* the other man to say the wrong thing. "Go ahead."

Their battlefield would be of his choosing, not Fargo's. "When I have the right questions," he told the chief mildly, "I'll be sure to come look you up."

Fargo's eyes narrowed into pale blue slits. "You do that." He shifted his gaze to Carly, who had been, for the most part, silently witnessing this exchange. Though there was a smile on the older man's lips, he looked far from happy. "Looks like recess time is over, Ms. Finn." He waved at the children behind her. "You'd best get those little ones back to their classrooms."

It was a veiled order, and Carly knew it. Nodding, she let the chief think that she appreciated his prompting. There was no point in digging in now. She needed Fargo to believe she was as mindless as all the other women who had chosen to cleave to Grayson's remodeled version of paradise on earth.

"Right you are, Chief."

Turning, she deliberately avoided making eye contact with Hawk, afraid he would see too much there, things that would give him pause. Because if he thought that what she was doing might all be an act, she was certain that Fargo, who was smarter than he actually looked, would pick up on it.

Worse, the chief might act on it. She didn't want any harm coming to Hawk. Though it might sound callous to someone else, she didn't care about the women whose murders were being investigated. They were dead, and nothing would change that. But Hawk wasn't. She didn't want Hawk getting hurt, and if he stayed here any length of time, he just might become a target.

It wasn't safe here anymore.

Hawk had always shot straight from the hip, and around here, that was dangerous. Fargo wasn't a man to cross and neither was Grayson or any of his cold-blooded henchmen. The only way to deal with any of them was to pretend to play the game.

As Carly withdrew, Fargo remained standing where he was, his right hand resting on the hilt of his holstered weapon as he regarded Hawk.

"Anything else I can do for you?" Fargo asked.

Hawk knew the value of retreat in order to regroup for another time, another battle. "I'll let you know, Chief," he promised noncommittally, just before he turned and walked away.

"You won't have any trouble finding me," Fargo called after him. "I patrol these streets pretty regularly. Seeing me among 'em is what keeps folks on the straight and narrow."

"Got it," Hawk replied without bothering to turn around. He did his best not to sound dismissive.

When he had initially left town, he remembered that Fargo had been a deputy, not the sheriff and certainly nothing as pretentious sounding as "chief of police." In addition, the man had also been the town bully, more given to causing trouble than to quelling it. Fargo took over, according to the information that he'd collected, when the old sheriff died in a freak accident.

He wondered just how much of it had been an accident and how much had involved a freak. Might just be something else to investigate, Hawk thought, after he cleared up this matter of the five women's murders.

Crossing to his car, Hawk blew out a breath. Just what the hell had happened here in the past five years or so? Five years was also about the time that the first body had turned up. And *that* coincided with another piece of information that the Bureau had discovered about Grayson and his band of not-so-merry-men. They had descended on the town, under the guise of being business "investors," and started buying up property with the intention of making renovations five years ago.

He'd read the reports that had been compiled, but he'd never dreamed the extent to which all this actually went. Grayson had transformed everything, as well as everyone he encouraged to remain in the town, creating what he freely touted as being "paradise on earth."

There was no such thing and they all knew it, Hawk thought, getting into his car. Or were supposed to know it.

After closing the door, he fastened his seat belt. What Grayson had really created was a town of zombies. Key in hand, Hawk remained sitting in his car, observing the people on Main Street for a few more minutes. He was acutely aware that Fargo was watching him watch the good citizens of Cold Plains.

It struck him in less than another minute that there was something *really* wrong with this scenario, something that went beyond the inane smiles and the overly neat clothing. Didn't anyone get dirty anymore? Not even the kids? What he noticed was that there wasn't a single neutral expression in the whole lot.

It wasn't possible for *everyone* to actually be happy at the same time, just as it wasn't possible that they all looked so perfect. No one was limping or stumbling, no one was coughing or sneezing. What the hell had the great God Grayson done, outlawed allergies, colds and imperfections? Had the man also managed to outlaw plain people? Because there were no plain people on these streets, certainly not ugly people, at least as far as his eye could see.

Something was very, very wrong here.

Fargo, apparently, had decided to surrender his passive role as observer, because the man was now on the move, heading straight for him, Hawk realized. In response, Hawk switched on his ignition and started his car.

For now, he wanted to get back to the cabin outside of town to make sure that the task force he'd put together was settled in. He'd picked good people, but he had an uneasy feeling that before this was over, they would need reinforcements.

Lots of them.

Carly could feel her insides shaking.

From the first floor window of her classroom, she'd covertly watched Fargo and Hawk regarding one another, two stags about to lock horns. She'd prayed that Hawk would have the good sense to leave before something bad happened.

When Fargo started walking toward Hawk, she thought her pounding heart would break one of her ribs. Fargo was like a bull moose and Hawk—Hawk was too damn stubborn for his own good. He might be the younger of the two, but the Hawk she remembered didn't fight dirty. He was nothing if not honorable. Fargo wasn't shackled by any such noble conventions. To Fargo, the prime directive was to get rid of any obstacles that might get in his way and those who might ultimately impede Samuel's control over Cold Plains.

Oh God, the sooner she could get Mia out of here, the better, she thought, still watching the two men. Desperation stole over her when she thought of Mia. Her sister wouldn't listen to reason. That left having to find a way to kidnap her, to drag Mia kicking and screaming out of Cold Plains before she was forced to marry that man.

Brice Carrington had been married once before, and no one knew exactly what had happened to the first Mrs. Carrington, other than the fact that one day, Carrington had haltingly announced that she was "gone from this earth."

Just like that, the woman was no longer among the living. Not unlike, Carly recalled, what had happened to the chief of police's wife. She had disappeared, as well, making Bo Fargo a widower—or so the man had claimed. No one really questioned him about it. One day the man was married, then the next day, he wasn't.

It occurred to Carly that the men in Cold Plains did not get divorced. If they found themselves suddenly alone and widowers, it was because they had conveniently "lost" their wives.

What if these women were not "lost" but rather eliminated? What if Carrington's wife and the chief's wife had been killed, just like those five women whose deaths Hawk was investigating?

And what if there were a lot more dead women buried throughout the state, women who had come from Cold Plains and who, for one reason or another, had fallen out of favor with Samuel?

Now that she thought of it, Carly vaguely remembered hearing someone say that Brice Carrington had wanted children to carry on his legacy and the first Mrs. Carrington hadn't been able to have any children. Was that her sin? The inability to conceive and produce little disciples for Grayson? Was *that* why Carrington was marrying Mia, so she could become the baby machine he both wanted and expected?

Oh, Mia, Mia, how can you be so blind? They just want to use you. And you're letting them.

"Is something wrong, Carly?"

The question, coming from behind her and quietly worded, nearly caused Carly to jump out of her skin. Even at its lowest point, it struck her as a very creepy-sounding voice.

Samuel.

Looking out the window, she hadn't heard him come into her classroom. The man moved like smoke—or like the devil, except that his cloven hooves were muted, hidden inside of hand-stitched shoes, which cost more than a lot of the farmers and the ranchers in the area managed to earn in any given year.

Samuel Grayson, movie-star handsome, with a tongue that was smoother than sweetened whipped cream, and blessed with hypnotic eyes that could easily hold a soul in place, had left the tiny town of Horn's Gulf years ago to make his mark—and his money—as a motivational speaker.

Increasingly more and more successful, he toured the Southwest and gave seminars to hapless people who wanted nothing more than to be half as dynamic as the man who had captured their attention and fired up their souls.

So they plunked their money down and listened in rapt attention, hoping for miracles to strike, miracles that would transform them into veritable clones of the stirring speaker. And as they prayed, Grayson went about the business of separating these desperate would-be disciples of his from their "contributions."

Contributions, Carly knew, a good many of them could ill afford to give. But that didn't bother—or stop—Grayson from collecting what he obviously felt was his due.

Eventually he grew bored and sought new challenges. Not content with moving from city to city, reaping money and unconditional adulation, Grayson had apparently decided to return to his roots and seek out a place to transform and make his own. A place that appeared to be dying. Cold Plains fit the bill.

Whether his own motivation came out of a desire to revenge himself on someone or from a need to come full circle and take over a town that reminded him of the place where he'd once been regarded as a ne'er do well, she didn't know and, frankly, she didn't care. What mattered was that he hadn't sucked her into his vortex no matter how hard he had tried.

The meaningless, empty smile she'd displayed for Hawk earlier curved her lips now as she looked up at the man who professed to being the town's "gentle, guiding conscience."

"No, Mr. Grayson," she replied politely, "nothing's wrong."

Grayson surprised her by slipping his arm around her shoulders in a familiar manner she instantly resented. Carly could feel herself screaming on the inside. But she didn't have that luxury right now, nor could she shrug him off—or push him away—the way she would have so much preferred.

"Now Carly," Grayson chided, "what was it I told you?" He looked at her pointedly.

For a second, because she was still recovering from the absolute shock of seeing Hawk back in Cold Plains, Carly's mind went blank.

And then she realized what Grayson was so coyly referring to.

"You said to call you Samuel."

"Yes, I did. There is no hierarchy here," he assured her, an insincere smile vouching for the veracity of his statement.

The hell there isn't, and you know it, Carly thought as she deliberately mirrored the smile on Grayson's thin, pursed lips.

"Now come on," he coaxed, "let me hear you say it."

"There's nothing wrong, *Samuel,*" Carly repeated sweetly.

Samuel made a show of peering into her eyes, as if

he was looking into her soul, as well. It was all part of the act, and they both knew it, Carly thought.

"Are you sure now, Carly?" Grayson asked solicitously. Then before she could reply again, he continued, "I thought what with Hawk's unexpected return here to Cold Plains, you might find yourself having to deal with some 'issues' the two of you might have had." He singled out the word, emphasizing it like a television pop psychologist.

That blindsided her.

There were times when the man really did seem to know everything, Carly thought uneasily. At those times she could almost believe Grayson *was* omnipotent, the way some of his followers claimed.

But no man was, and Grayson was definitely *not* the exception but the rule.

"No, I'm fine. Really. Hawk and I were over a long time ago," she told him staunchly.

Grayson nodded, his expression unreadable and all the more unnerving because of that. She didn't know if he believed her or was just playing her.

"That's good," he replied in a tone that equally revealed nothing. "But if you ever find yourself wanting to talk or just in need of a friendly, nonjudgmental ear, my door is always open," he told her, punctuating his words with a warm squeeze of her shoulders, which was hardly quick in nature.

It took everything she had not to allow her revulsion to show through.

Instead, Carly forced herself to assume a beaming,

grateful expression. "Thank you, Samuel. You're very kind."

"I can be kinder," he assured her, his voice pulsing with promise as their eyes met.

Not even if hell freezes over and the fate of the world depended on it, she thought.

Any second now, she was positive she would throw up. Time to retreat.

"I'd better be getting back to the children," she told Grayson. She gestured toward the rows of eerily quiet seven-year-olds who were sitting at their desks, their hands folded. "I can only count on their behaving themselves for just so long."

Grayson's magnetic green eyes met hers. "I was just thinking the same thing."

Carly knew that she had just been put on notice. If she was going to get Mia out of here, it would have to be soon.

Very soon.

Chapter 5

Thinking that their conversation was over, Carly hoped that Grayson would finally leave the classroom. But the self-appointed leader of the renovated Cold Plains community made no move to walk out. Instead, the man remained where he was, uncomfortably close to her.

Carly instinctively braced herself for round two.

"You know, your sister is coming along very well," Grayson said. "She is going to be a fine addition to our peaceful, little community once she and Brice are finally married."

Every word out of Grayson's mouth sounded so terribly wrong to her, especially this. After going through the motions of this charade she was forced to play for the past couple of months, if the man had said that the grass was green, she would have expected to look down and see that, instead of green, it was actually a shade of blue.

Wanting desperately to point out how horribly patronizing and chauvinistic he sounded, Carly bit her tongue, swallowing the hot words that instantly rose to her lips. Instead, she forced herself to say what she knew Grayson was waiting to hear.

"I haven't had much time to talk with Mia," she told him, "but I know that she's very excited about the wedding."

"The ceremony's only three weeks away," Grayson needlessly reminded her.

Or was he actually just goading her? With him it was difficult to tell. The only thing she would have sworn to was that there wasn't a drop of human kindness in the man's entire body. Not only that, but he was lecherous, as well. She'd seen the way Grayson looked at some of the women in the community, married and unmarried alike. The look in his eyes definitely did *not* belong to a man who was "pure of heart," the way he claimed.

Somehow, she managed to keep her vacant smile in place. "Yes, I know."

Just how much longer was she going to have to pretend that Grayson wasn't looking at her right now as if she were a piece of barbecued meat and he hadn't eaten in a month?

Mia, think of Mia. You tell this charlatan what you think of him, and Mia's lost.

Carly curled her fingers into her palms, digging her nails in to keep from saying something that would make her feel better but would ultimately ruin everything.

"You know, you might think about finding some-one and getting married yourself, Carly," Grayson sug-gested. She could almost *feel* his eyes touching her. "After all, at thirty-one you must be hearing your prime reproductive minutes ticking loudly away."

If she were having a normal conversation with a normal, albeit opinionated and annoying, man, she would have been tempted to haul off and hit him for the demeaning way he was talking to her. But giving in to her more primitive instincts wasn't going to help rescue Mia. So again, Carly forced herself to pretend to agree with him.

"Actually, I do, but so far, there hasn't been anyone I would want to spend the rest of my life with."

Grayson waved away the excuse. "Nonsense, I know plenty of eligible men I can introduce you to. You're just being too picky, Carly," he chided, although he contin-ued to smile at her. "But I do sense a certain wavering within you," he confessed. "It's only natural," he as-sured her. "Some people come to the right path after taking all the wrong ones, and they can't bring them-selves to believe they've finally found the right road. I could give you some private lessons if you like," he of-fered. "Share with you the benefits of all I've seen and learned about this way of life."

Though she gave no outward indication, Carly was instantly on her guard. They were shadow boxing. She could sense it. Grayson was trying to make her slip up, to let her true intentions show through.

Don't hold your breath, Grayson. I've fooled a better man than you, she thought, remembering the look on Hawk's face when she told him she really didn't love him.

"I couldn't impose on you that way." Carly paused a moment, then added his name to her declaration, enunciating it slowly, melodically, "Samuel. You're much too busy a man. I'd feel guilty taking up your time like that."

He laughed off her protest. "I'm never too busy to spend some quality time with one of the community's good citizens, Carly." His peppermint-laced breath seemed to form a cloud all around her, making it difficult to breathe. "You'll find, my dear, that I can be *very* approachable."

Yes, she just bet he could be. She'd heard that he had "approached" at least half a dozen women within the transformed sectors of Cold Plains since she began paying attention to what was happening here, to the place she called home.

"I shall keep that in mind," she promised. "But now I really do need to get back to my lesson plan." She smiled up sweetly at him, entertaining herself with the thought that some day that man would get what was coming to him. And maybe having Hawk here signaled the beginning of the end of King Samuel's would-be reign. She relished the thought. "Otherwise," she continued, "the children won't be able to do their homework assignments tonight."

"Careful, Carly," he warned with a warm smile. "You don't want the little ones thinking that you're a slave driver."

Instead of just being enslaved by a man with a golden

tongue, she countered silently. Because that was what Grayson did, enslave an entire community of people who now moved about like automatons, with compliant, moronic smiles on their faces.

Were all the people here so easily brainwashed? Were they all so desperate for something new, something different, something supposedly "better" that they would blindly obey a man whose real agenda was still hidden?

The thought made her very uneasy—as did the realization that she wasn't really safe. Grayson had all but put her on notice. She would have to be on her guard against him. No doubt, he had plans for her, plans that very well just might make her wind up the same way that those five women whose bodies were scattered throughout the state had ultimately wound up.

She had no proof, but in her heart, Carly just *knew* those dead women were somehow tied to Grayson.

She also knew she should be afraid, really afraid, but somehow, just knowing that Hawk was in the area quelled her uneasiness. He'd always had the ability to make her feel safe. Maybe it was unrealistic to think that he still gave a damn what happened to her, but somehow, she sensed that he did.

The children, thirty seven- and eight-year-olds in total, finally began to grow restless. Had they been a normal bunch they would have gotten that way much sooner.

For now, she turned her attention to them, putting any and all thoughts of Grayson, Mia and Hawk on the back burner. Or at least trying to.

She was successful on two counts, but Hawk's image refused to take a backseat to *anything*.

Two out of three wasn't bad, Carly consoled herself.

The minute he'd driven away from the center of town—and away from Fargo's steely gaze—Hawk pulled over to the side of the road and took out his cell phone. By now he knew the number by heart.

Punching the numbers in, he tried to reach Micah Grayson again. He'd been trying the number periodically ever since the man hadn't shown up for their appointment or called to explain why.

And as with all the other times when he actually *could* get through—and reception out here left a great deal to be desired—Hawk heard the phone on the other end ring once, then immediately after that heard his call go to voice mail.

There was no need to leave yet another message. He'd already left three. Still, Hawk bit off, "Where the hell are you, Grayson? I swear, if you're not dead, you will be."

With that, he jabbed at the word *End* on his phone and terminated his unsuccessful call before jamming the cell phone back into his pocket.

Sitting there, he impatiently drummed his fingers on the dashboard. Ordinarily, he wasn't a man who worried. He just calculated worst-case scenario and the probability percentages that such a scenario would actually occur. But the problem was that this time he *was* worried. Really worried. Micah Grayson was nothing if not a consummate professional and completely business oriented, even though the business he was in was utterly unorthodox.

In the old tradition, Micah was as good as his word, which was his bond. If he had said he'd show up somewhere, then he'd show up. Unless something really dire had happened to him, preventing him from keeping the appointment.

And if that was the case, had this "dire something" happened because of his chosen occupation, or was it somehow tied to what Micah wanted to tell him about the murdered women?

Since there were no answers right now, why should he make himself crazy? Hawk thought. There was already enough of that going on. His mind reverted back to his last exchange with Carly in the school yard.

Damn but this land, which was cruel and hard on everyone, had somehow been good to her. She'd lost weight, he'd observed. Just enough weight to make her hauntingly beautiful, not enough to make her appear weathered and worn.

There was no justice in the world, he thought. If there was, he would have found her off-putting and frazzled, with a pack of little kids squabbling at her feet.

But that, he reminded himself, would have meant that someone had to have been with her. Touching her. Making love to her. And that would have clearly torn him apart.

Was this any better? he silently demanded. Seeing her and finding out that he still wanted her? Maybe more than ever?

His cell phone began ringing. It took him a couple

of rings to extract it from his pocket again. Glancing at the number, he realized that he was still nursing the hope that Micah would turn up as mysteriously as he'd vanished and call back.

But the caller wasn't Micah, it was Boyd Patterson, one of the three special agents he'd recruited for this mission.

"Bledsoe," Hawk snapped as he answered his phone. In return, he heard a high-pitched noise on the other end, followed by static and then a voice that sounded as if it actually belonged to an extraterrestrial attempting to make first contact. "Patterson?" Hawk asked dubiously. Other than the caller ID on his screen, he hadn't heard anything to correctly identify the person on the other end of his squawking phone.

In response to his single word question, Hawk heard more static, now joined by an ear-shattering crackling noise.

Civilization, he thought in frustration, was still only moderately flirting with places like Cold Plains. Full contact with the inventions of the past ten years was still a patience-trying league away.

"Listen, I can't hear you," Hawk finally said into the phone, raising his voice in case the reception on Patterson's end was better than what he was hearing on his. There was no point in continuing to try to make out what, if anything, was being said on the other end of this call. "If this *is* Patterson, I'm about fifteen minutes out and heading back to the cabin. Stop draining the damn battery and turn your cell off for now. Maybe you'll have better luck using it later."

With that, Hawk ended his call and instead of putting the cell phone back into his jacket pocket, he tossed the small smartphone onto the passenger seat, leaving it within easy reach in case a miracle happened and decent reception actually put in a public appearance for more than a ten-second spate.

The phone remained silent for the duration of his trip.

It wound up taking him less than the promised fifteen minutes to reach the secluded cabin. He'd already been here a number of times to check out its accessibility as well as to ascertain just how much visibility was available from within the cabin. He wanted no surprises—just in case he and his team needed to make a stand here.

To the untrained eye, the modest little cabin looked like the perfect getaway home, a place where a busy executive might take off for a few days to unwind and become one with nature.

What it *didn't* look like was a place where four FBI special agents were conducting an investigation into Samuel Grayson's comings and goings, his land holdings as well as the "investors" he had brought along with him. All this while actively maintaining surveillance on the man and his main residence.

The cabin's rustic appearance suited Hawk's purposes just fine.

Though there was no one in the area, Hawk left nothing to chance and was not about to drop his guard or grow lax. He parked his vehicle behind the cabin, out of sight. The other three agents, he noted with approval, had already done the same. If someone did happen to drive by in the coming days, nothing out front would arouse curiosity or create the need for speculation.

Walking into the three-room cabin through the rear door he'd had put in, Hawk was instantly enveloped in a warm, welcoming scent. One of the agents was cooking. Unless he missed his guess, the agent was making stew. The tempting aroma reminded him that he hadn't really eaten today. Seeing Carly again had thrown him off and killed his appetite. Things like food and eating had temporarily been banished to a nether region.

But now hunger returned, barreling through him with a vengeance. He could hear his stomach growling, making demands.

He passed the agent who had been on the other end of the unsuccessful call. Special agent Boyd Patterson looked as if he was currently at his wit's end, trying to coax a little cooperation from his Bureau-issued laptop.

"Smells good," Hawk commented, nodding toward the tiny kitchen in the rear.

The other agent barely glanced up. "Rosenbloom bought supplies," he explained, preoccupied. "He figured since we're going to be stuck here, he might as well make us all something decent to eat."

Hawk smiled, nodding his approval. "Knew I brought him along for a reason." Then he raised his voice and called out to the rear of the cabin, "Someday you're going to make some woman a wonderful wife, Rosy."

Lawrence Rosenbloom paused momentarily to stick his head out of the alcove. The tall, thin special agent had initially trained to become a world-class top chef before he'd succumbed to the enticing, so-called promise of adventure and excitement while in the service of his country.

He took his superior's comment in stride, firing back, "I'd be careful what I said, Bledsoe. When I worked at a famous five-star restaurant in New York, I saw servers spit into the food they were bringing out to customers who irritated them."

Hawk nodded, as if this revelation was news to him. "Any of these customers have a gun?" he asked the other agent mildly.

Rosenbloom went back to slowly stirring his creation. "Can't say that I ever saw any."

"Therein lies the difference," Hawk told him, his voice still incredibly friendly. "*I* have a gun. I ever catch you even thinking about doing what you just said, I'll use it."

"Point taken." Rosenbloom grinned. "Guess that makes this a standoff."

"Guess so," Hawk agreed.

"So?" Patterson interrupted impatiently. He wasn't one of those types who regarded camping as something even remotely recreational. He preferred skyscrapers to grass every time. "Did you find out anything?" he asked with interest.

Yeah, I found out I'm still in love with Carly Finn even after all these years. I found out I'm not the robot I thought I was. And it sucks!

Out loud, Hawk replied, "Yeah, I found out something. I don't know *why* Samuel Grayson came in with his men and bought up huge chunks of property, but he's managed to turn the whole damn town into the movie set straight out of *The Stepford Wives.*"

Patterson blinked, trying to follow what he was being told. But Hawk had lost him with the reference. "The what?"

"It's a cult classic," Rosenbloom's disembodied voice came floating out of the kitchen alcove. "All the wives in Stepford were brainwashed into being obedient and subservient to their husbands. They moved around the town like a bunch of smiling, mindless robots."

Temporarily pushing back from the table and his computer, Patterson grinned. "Sounds great. Where do I sign up?"

"Spoken like a man who hasn't been married," the third agent, Stephen Jeffers, a twenty-year veteran both of the Bureau and marriage, remarked. There was a note of pity in his voice.

Taking a momentary break, Rosenbloom left the stove and walked out into the main room. "If that's all you want out of a relationship, Patterson, get yourself a dog from an animal shelter. Me, I like intelligent conversation and a woman with some proven fighting spirit."

The grin on Patterson's face turned wistful as he allowed his mind to drift for a second. It was a general known fact that Rosenbloom's wife was not just intelligent and feisty, she was exceedingly sexy, as well.

"Spirit sounds good," Patterson agreed.

"Right about now, *anything* sounds good to him, Bledsoe," Rosenbloom explained as he turned back to the meal that was almost ready. "I think he's getting cabin fever."

Patterson had been the last of the four of them to arrive here.

"After only twelve hours?" Hawk asked incredulously. They hadn't even gotten their feet wet yet. And while he was hoping that he could find enough evidence to quickly wrap up the case, he was too realistic to pin his hopes on that.

"Doesn't take long," Patterson volunteered. "You forget, I'm a city boy. What the hell do people do around here for entertainment—besides watching paint dry and grass grow, I mean."

"I don't know about 'other people,'" Hawk told him, "but you're going over anything we can find on Samuel Grayson. That includes his background from the minute he was born as well as the people he's associated with since then."

Patterson glanced toward the front window, and Hawk could almost read the other man's mind.

"And under no circumstances," he went on to warn, "are you or Rosy or Jeffers to go into Cold Plains. Strangers stand out like sore thumbs there. I don't want Grayson getting it into his head that I didn't come alone." They didn't have much going for them, so this at least gave them the element of surprise if they needed it. Every little bit helped.

"What about supplies?" Rosenbloom wanted to know. "I can't make this stew last for more than a couple of days, Hawk."

"No one's asking for the miracle of the fishes and

the loaves," Hawk replied, walking into the alcove for a moment. He nodded at the stove. "Where'd you get those?"

"Little town thirty miles south of here," Rosenbloom answered. "Hadleyville, I think it was called."

The name sounded vaguely familiar to him. "Then that's where you'll go to get anything else. Cold Plains is full of grinning zombies. I could use a little leverage on my side, and it looks like you three are going to be it."

"Zombies?" Patterson questioned with a touch of confusion.

Hawk snorted. "They might as well be. From what I saw, they look like the only thoughts they had in their heads were the ones put there by Grayson."

"Is everyone on board with this guy?" Patterson wanted to know.

"That's what I intend to find out," Hawk answered, then added with a grin, "After I have some of Rosy's stew, of course."

"Coming right up, Fearless Leader," Rosenbloom sang out. The next minute, he walked into the living room, using a makeshift tray he'd created out of a board of wood to carry four bowls of hot stew.

The warm meal didn't quite wipe away the cold, tight knot that had formed in Hawk's stomach the moment he had seen Carly, but he had to admit that it did help. Some. At least he now felt ready to face the very definite possibility of seeing her again.

Chapter 6

A week went by.

A week involving what turned out to be mostly painstakingly fruitless observations and smoldering, growing frustration. Though he would have been the first to say he'd severed all ties to Cold Plains, the truth was that Hawk did *not* like what he saw happening within the town he'd once called home. The more he watched, the more annoyed he became.

He grew more convinced that, at the very least, Samuel Grayson was out to line his own pockets at the expense of the weak-minded sheep who had so easily fallen under his spell. It was as if they had no backbone, no will of their own.

He continued to try Micah's number at least once a day, with the same frustrating results. Micah wasn't picking up and he was nowhere to be found.

Hawk's bad feeling continued to escalate.

He and the three special agents who comprised his team went on gathering information both on Grayson and on anyone in the man's employ. They relied on both covert, firsthand observations as well as doing intense research as they went over old records and current databases.

Every night, before he finally returned to his hotel room in town, a hotel room he was certain Grayson had bugged, Hawk would find himself driving over to the farm where Carly still lived.

The farm that had come between them because she had remained to operate it for her father and sister, and he had left to find his true destiny.

All the other nights, he had just driven past it, glancing to see if the lights were on.

They always were.

But tonight, tonight was different. Instead of continuing on his way, he'd stopped. Not slowed down as he'd initially intended, but stopped dead. He turned off his engine.

Hawk leaned back in the driver's seat, willing the knots out of his shoulders. He told himself that he was here because he had questions for her. Questions about what was going on in town. Questions that pertained to the five murdered women.

After all, if she hadn't left town, hadn't moved on in all this time, who better to talk to about Cold Plains and the changes that had taken place than Carly? She was an observant woman, she should have insight into these things. The fact that he'd had feelings for her shouldn't matter.

Shouldn't.

But it did.

Because he still had feelings for her. He hadn't realized just how much or how strong until the second he'd seen her a week ago.

Hell, the whole damn world had just stopped dead on its axis, freezing in place. The only sound he'd heard for a split second was the sound of his own heart banging against his rib cage, fit to kill.

So much for telling himself that he was over her. That he would *ever* be over her, for that matter.

Hawk squared his shoulders. Well, he wouldn't get any questions answered like this, sitting inside his car, watching darkness creep in and surround her house.

He allowed anger to get the better of him. It got his blood pumping, and that, in turn, forced him to get out of the car.

She'd been home for over half an hour now. That was how long he'd sat out there, watching the house. Debating his next move.

He'd followed her from the school, where she'd remained far longer than her students had. Though he told himself not to be, he had been consumed with curiosity about what she was doing and what had kept her there until almost seven, practically four hours after parents and school buses had shown up to transport students back to their homes. Was she grading papers? Talking to other teachers?

Spending time with Grayson?

A flash of something hot, unwieldy and unreasonable shot through him. Hawk refused to identify or put a label on it. Jealousy was for other people, not him. Certainly not now.

For a second, he focused on Grayson. He knew that Samuel Grayson and Micah, his missing informant, were twins, and at first glance, the two men did look alike. But while Micah was a natural for his chosen line of work, a methodical, keenly observant man of few words who could terminate a man's existence with a minimum of moves, Samuel was outgoing, gregarious and not only played up but relied on his looks.

No matter how you dressed him up, Samuel Grayson still reminded him of a snake oil salesman. And from what he'd heard, Grayson actually *was* selling something. Grayson had his people collecting, bottling and preparing half liter bottles of "healing" tonic water.

The water in question came from the creek behind the community center. Legend had it that the water had immense healing powers and that, some said, it actually had some of the elements of a fountain of youth in it, as well.

Bottles of this "healing water" were placed on sale— "offered" at twenty-five dollars a pop—in the community center. The water that flowed in the creek was no longer available to the citizens of Cold Plains except through Grayson. He had seen to that, buying the land on both sides of the creek and turning it into private property.

Not only were bottles placed on sale independently, but they were also on sale at the weekly seminars that he gave. Regular attendance was mandatory if those in his flock wanted to remain in good standing with both Grayson and the rest of the "community." Purchase of the bottled water was mandatory, as well. And with each purchase, Grayson's coffers became a little fuller.

The man had a hell of a racket going for him, Hawk couldn't help thinking. He could understand how a lot of the people who lived here had gotten ensnared. They'd been trapped by dreams of well-being and contentment that Grayson seemed to be able to market so effortlessly. The people of Cold Plains had had so very little to cling to, and Grayson dealt in hope. Albeit unrealistic hope, but when a person was truly desperate, any hope was better than none at all.

That was their excuse, he thought, dismissing the other citizens he'd seen herded into Grayson's "meeting center." But what was hers?

Carly had never been a woman to wallow in self-pity or one who allowed herself to be sidelined or defeated by dwelling on worst-case scenarios. When they were growing up, she had always been the one to buoy him up, to make him feel as if he could put up with it all, because there was a better life waiting for him—for them—on the horizon.

Granted she'd dashed it all by telling him that the one thing he had clung to—that she loved him—was a lie. But even that wouldn't explain why she had been transformed from an independent, intelligent young woman to an obedient, mindless robot.

He couldn't have been *that* wrong about her, Hawk told himself.

Finally climbing out of the car, Hawk resisted the temptation to slam the door in his wake. Instead, he merely closed it, then strode over to her front door—just the way he had done so very many times in the past.

He ached for things that lay buried deep in years gone by.

Hawk rang the bell—and heard nothing. No one had ever gotten around to fixing the doorbell, he realized. It had been broken when he used to call on her.

Some things never changed.

Too bad that other things did.

Raising his hand, he knocked on the door. Then goaded by impatience, he knocked again. He'd just raised his hand to knock for a third time when the door finally opened.

Carly, with her hair pinned back from her face, stood in the doorway. She wore frayed jeans and a T-shirt that had seen one too many washings.

She'd never looked more beautiful to him.

He saw surprise, instantly followed by uneasiness, pass over her face. Her eyes darted from one side to the other, as if checking the area. Then rather than asking him what he was doing here or what he wanted, she ordered sharply, "Get inside," and stepped to one side to give him access.

All but yanking him in, she scanned the darkening, flat terrain one last time, then quickly closed the door behind him.

Whirling around to face Hawk, she finally spoke. "What are you doing here?"

The question was tersely asked and no empty, mindless smile accompanied her words. She wasn't smiling at all. Instead, she appeared agitated.

That was more like it, he thought. But was she agitated? Did it have to do with finding him here—or was Grayson behind her display of uneasiness?

"What the hell is going on here?" he demanded. "And what the hell happened to you?"

"You don't answer a question with more questions," she informed him, snapping out her words. It was a defense mechanism. Because she was afraid where this would wind up taking her.

Taking them.

"I don't want an English lesson or a grammar lesson, Carly," he retorted in the same exasperated tone she had just used. "I want an answer."

All promises to hold on to his temper had flown out the proverbial window. He cut the distance between them from several feet down to less than a few inches.

He was in her space and she in his, and the air turned hot and sultry between them, despite the fact that outside, the April night was crisp and clean. And more than a little cold.

"Damn it, Carly," he shouted at her, "this isn't you."

"This is me," she countered stubbornly.

Hawk's brown eyes darkened as they narrowed. "I refuse to believe that."

"Well, unfortunately for you, you don't have a say in it. It is what it is, no matter what you say to the contrary," she maintained stubbornly. "Besides, you've been gone for ten years, you have no idea what kind of transformations have been going on and taking place here," she pointed out.

"Maybe not." He agreed to the general principle she'd raised. "The town looks like it's gone to hell in that handbasket our grandmothers were always talking about."

She would have smiled if this wasn't so serious. "The town has prospered," she contradicted, dutifully spouting the party line. For all she knew, he was now in Grayson's employ, too. He was out here to trip her up for some reason she hadn't figured out yet. "Just look around the next time you're on Main Street."

"I have." His expression told her that he was far from impressed with the changes. She would have been—had they not come at such a high price. "It's like they all made a deal with the devil." He paused, his eyes pinning her. "Did you do that, too, Carly? Did you make a deal with the devil?"

She should have taken it as a compliment, because it meant that she was playing her role well and was convincing. But instead, she felt insulted that he thought so little of her.

Isn't that what you wanted? To come across as one of Grayson's mindless minions?

The answer was that she both wanted it, and she didn't. A part of her felt he should have known better than to think this of her.

Her feelings were getting in the way of her common sense and her plan.

She tossed her head, her eyes blazing. "I don't know what you're talking about."

Carly began to turn her back on him, but he caught her by the wrist, holding her in place. "I think you do," he told her.

"What you think really doesn't matter to me," she lied, doing her best to ignore the wild turmoil going on in the pit of her stomach. She attempted to pull free but only succeeded in having him tighten his hold on her. "You're hurting me," she accused.

"Am I?" he retorted angrily. "Am I hurting you?" Struggling with himself, he opened his hand and released her. Anger continued to flash in his eyes. "Well, it's nothing compared to what you did to me."

Carly raised her chin contentiously. "I didn't hurt you, Hawk," she informed him. "What I did was set you free."

Had she lost her mind? Did living under Grayson's thumb completely destroy her ability to think? "What are you talking about?"

After all this time, she would have thought it might have dawned on him. Apparently not. She spelled it out as much as she could.

"You left here to become something. To make something of yourself. To follow your dream. And from what I can see, you succeeded. So in the long run, you should actually be grateful to me. Because of me," she concluded, "you got to be happy."

How the hell had she come to that conclusion? "Wrong on both counts," he told her, cynicism clinging to every syllable.

He was just saying that to get back at her for hurting his male pride by rejecting her all those years ago.

Couldn't see the forest for the trees, could he? Neither could he see what her sacrifice had ultimately cost her. Maybe he wasn't as smart as she'd initially thought.

"But this is what you wanted, isn't it?" she pressed, trying to get him to admit it. "Authority, adventure, moving from place to place, making a difference. Helping people." She repeated to him everything he had once told her.

At the top of his list had been leaving Cold Plains. Well, she'd gotten him to do that. The rest, she'd assumed at the time, had followed and fallen into place. Finding out he was an FBI special agent just reinforced that for her.

"What I wanted," he shouted hoarsely into Carly's face, unable to hold himself in check any longer, "was you!"

She didn't believe him. Because if that were true, she would have never been able to get him to leave, no matter what lie she told him. Or, if he'd left, he would have come back in a short time, saying something about being determined to get her to change her mind—or words to that effect.

But he *had* left and he *hadn't* returned, not for ten years, and now it was a case that brought Hawk back, not her.

"Let's see." She raised her right hand as if she was cupping some invisible object, weighing it. "Me," she announced, nodding at her hand. Then Carly raised her other hand for a moment. "Versus a lifetime of adventure and achievement." She indicated that what her left hand was holding was heavier by letting it sink a lot lower than her right hand. "Doesn't seem like much of a contest to me."

Hawk took hold of her hand in his, pulling her in and eliminating the last tiny bit of space that was still left between them. His eyes, blazing fiercely now, were on hers.

"No," he all but growled as he struggled to contain his temper and keep it from exploding. "It's not."

This time, she had a feeling that he wouldn't release her.

"Let go of me, Hawk," she ordered in a steely voice that gave no indication she was quaking on the inside. Her ability to hold him at bay, to resist her own mounting desires, quickly diminished. Any second now, it would all plummet to her feet.

Frustrated, worried, Carly made one last attempt to yank her wrist away from his grasp. She got nowhere. She might as well have been trying to pull it out of a bear trap. He had what amounted to a permanent hold on her.

"I said, let go!" she ground out between clenched teeth.

"Or what?" Hawk challenged. "You'll call Grayson and have him and his henchmen stick me into one of those unmarked graves he seems to favor so much?"

How can you even think that, you idiot? And then she thought of Mia and the very real danger her sister was in if this actually turned out to be true. Up until now, she'd thought of Grayson as a cold-blooded manipulator out for his own selfish interests. She hadn't thought of him as a killer.

This put a whole different, chilling spin on things.

"How do you know that Samuel's the one who is doing this?" she asked, wanting to hear his reasoning. She refrained from telling him her suspicions.

But Hawk noticed something else; something had caught his interest. She hadn't protested, hadn't cried out indignantly that Grayson would never be capable of such heinous actions.

Why?

Did she suspect that the former motivational speaker *was* behind it—or did she have information she wasn't telling him?

Open up to me, Carly. Trust me. You used to, remember?

Out loud he told her, "Grayson's the one who is obviously running the show here." He continued to hold her hand, afraid if he released it, she'd run off. And he wanted to hear the truth about this two-bit creep who'd hypnotized her into being one of the faithful—if not more. "He's a megalomaniac who's not about to allow anyone else to have any authority or share the spotlight with him. It's all about him, it always has been, always will be. And even though we haven't found the direct connection yet, every one of those five dead women— including the one without a name—lived in Cold Plains at one time or another."

With every passing second, her concern for Mia's safety grew. "How do you know that the woman without a name lived here?" she asked.

"That's on a need-to-know basis," Hawk retorted tersely. He grew acutely aware that he was still holding her wrist, acutely aware of how close they were. Just standing here like this was filling his senses with her very essence. "And you don't have a need to know," he informed her.

Her eyes met his. Though she didn't say a word, she pleaded with him silently, praying with all her heart that there was still a tiny trace of the connection that had once been so strong between them. The connection that allowed them to finish each other's sentences, to finish each other's thoughts.

Oh, but I do, Carly thought frantically. *I really do. I have a need to know* everything *that's involved in this case. Because Mia's life might just depend on it.*

Chapter 7

Hawk's deeply hypnotic eyes continued to hold her prisoner. Her nerves rose close to the surface and the very ground beneath her feet seemed to sink.

"I just can't figure out what you're still doing here," Hawk finally said. "Why you didn't leave when Grayson started buying up everything, changing everything? Turning people into grinning puppets?"

"Where would I go?" she asked. "This is *home.*"

"Where would you go?" Hawk echoed incredulously. "Anywhere is better than this." She had to see that. The Carly he knew was too smart to be taken in by the gingerbread, by the pretense. The Carly he remembered would be able to see that Grayson was not out for the greater good, but the greater haul—*for him.*

"First of all, I would *never* leave without Mia." He had to know that. "And she wants to stay here, and second, I can't just abandon Cold Plains because some silver-tongued Pied Piper decided to lay claim to it and would be changing things around."

Her description of Grayson was far from flattering, which immediately told him that unlike so many of the other town residents, she hadn't elevated the man to the level of a god. And the fiercely protective tone in her voice when she'd mentioned her sister gave him the hope that Mia was the real reason Carly was still here.

Which in turn meant that she hadn't fallen under the charlatan's spell, unlike Mia. This version of Carly at least bore some resemblance to the bright-eyed girl who had taken up so much space in his young life.

Hawk suppressed a sigh. He'd really thought that they were going to spend the rest of their lives together, grow old together. Funny how things turned out.

"So what's your plan?" he finally asked her. "Are you going to somehow covertly confront and then fight Grayson? Winner gets to keep Cold Plains, loser has to leave town, that kind of thing?"

Carly took offense at both the question and his tone. "You're making fun of me," she accused.

He thought of the way she'd been in the school yard that first day he returned to Cold Plains.

"No, I'm trying to understand why the spirited, feisty woman I once knew would allow herself to be ordered around like some mindless lackey. You can't possibly be taken in by Grayson's act. You're way too smart for that," Hawk insisted.

Despite the fact that she felt a very real desire to tell him what she was doing, maybe to ask for his help, she couldn't risk it. If this came to light, her chance of rescuing Mia would go down the drain.

So instead, she challenged, "Did you ever think that maybe you're being too cynical? That just maybe Samuel's on the level?"

A look of contempt came over his features. Whether it was directed at Grayson—or her—was difficult to tell from where she was standing.

"Yeah, and maybe the moon's made out of green cheese." His eyes narrowed to sharp green slits. "Look, I don't know what your so-called plan is, but I want you to stay away from Grayson, understand?" It wasn't a request, it was an order. "The man's dangerous."

She had *never* liked being ordered around, and now was no exception. "You have no right to waltz into town ten years after you left and think you can start telling me what to do."

The sharpness of her own reaction surprised her. Why was there this wealth of anger, of hurt, bubbling up within her? She had no right to resent him. After all, she had been the one to send him away. She'd been completely aware of what she was sacrificing, and she'd done it, anyway. Done it because she loved him. She couldn't resent him for doing exactly what she'd orchestrated for him to do—

And yet—

And yet, there was a part of her, a small, selfish, lost part of her, that had wanted him not to leave back then, no matter what she'd done to get him to go. Or, if he did go, she'd wanted him to dramatically return and announce that he wasn't going anywhere, not unless she came with him.

You can't fault him, she told herself sternly. *He'd tried. God knows, he'd tried. He even told you that he was willing to take Mia along when the two of you left town. It was your choice to stay, your choice because you thought that you and Mia were going to be like an anchor for him and his dreams, dragging him down.*

Besides, hadn't Hawk just admitted that what he'd wanted most in the world was her? What more did she want from the man? She was being irrational. But then, she'd heard that love did that to a person, made them entirely crazy and irrational. Made them want things that weren't possible.

Like living happily ever after.

"I'm a special agent with the FBI. I have every right to tell you what to do," he corrected, all but shouting into her face.

She felt no such need for restraint. "Go to hell," Carly shouted defiantly.

That tore it for him. The last fragile hold on his temper snapped like a dried twig underfoot after a long draught. "Not without you!"

The few seconds that followed were all a blur. What happened next was certainly not something he'd foreseen himself doing, even though, if he was being honest, it had taken place a thousand times in the half dreams that littered his mind, occurring just before dawn each morning.

One moment they were shouting at one another, their emotions completely exposed, raw and bleeding. The next, instead of shouting, he was kissing Carly with all the passion, the feelings that had just been uncovered and had spilled out.

And she was kissing him back with the same amount of verve.

The eruption was inevitable.

The magnitude of their emotions could only be contained for so long. The moment his lips touched hers, the second they came together, they both knew that there was no turning back. That whatever stories they had told themselves, saying their relationship had long been over, were all lies, pretenses to get them through the day, the week, the month. They'd all been very useful at the time, but still lies.

The moment they kissed, it was like two halves of a whole finally coming together. Like rain falling on a parched terrain to make it finally flourish again.

They *needed* one another to be complete.

God help her, she *needed* him.

Even though she knew she was going to regret this, knew that she should have remained strong and vigilant, she also knew that this was what she had been craving ever since she'd stood on the hill, keeping well out of sight, watching Hawk's car on the road that led away from town—away from *her*—grow smaller and smaller on the horizon.

She'd missed him since that moment, and if that was weak, well, so be it. She'd never claimed to be an invincible warrior.

Even though the tiny shred of common sense she still possessed told her to end this, to pull away, Carly couldn't help praying that this kiss would go on forever. Praying that he wouldn't abruptly pull back, look at her with perhaps a small trace of smugness and say something to the effect that he'd known all along that she still wanted him.

Because she did.

And this proved it beyond a shadow of a doubt. When it came to Hawk, she had no defenses, no resolve. No shame.

It was a terrible thing for Hawk to realize that after ten years of strict self-discipline that he couldn't even think straight.

Hell, he couldn't think at all.

Not a single thought that rose in his mind lived to see completion. Only broken fragments seemed to exist in his brain, and he swept those away, because they got in his way, got in the way of his being able to just savor this moment.

And if for some reason she was playing him for a fool, well then, he'd deal with that later. Right now, all he wanted to do was to fill his hands, his senses, his very *soul* with her. With the taste and feel of her.

With the very sound of her breathing, excitement radiating within each breath.

He was vaguely aware that they'd started out fully dressed, and then somewhere along the line, they weren't anymore. Whether she'd undressed him or he her—or they'd undressed one another or just themselves—none of that left an impression or even fleetingly registered in his memory bank.

None of that mattered.

What mattered, what left its indelible mark, was making love with her. What mattered was giving himself up to the heat, the passion, the demands that all but raged within him.

He couldn't get enough of her, but he kept trying.

He'd missed her, he admitted to himself, missed her the way he would have missed the very air had it been taken away from him.

Because in a way, it had.

Until this very moment.

Each soft curve that he touched, every pliant inch of skin he kissed brought back memories. Memories that had gone a long way in sustaining him.

And yet, somehow it almost felt as if this was the very first time he'd had her. He couldn't make sense of it, and he stopped trying. Stopped doing everything except enjoy her the way he'd yearned to for so long.

The very first time they had ever made love, they'd been in her father's barn, up in the hayloft. It was close to midnight, and moonlight had streamed in through the cracks in the uneven shutters, highlighting her face, adding to the glow that radiated from her.

Though each time they made love together had been special, he never forgot that first time. Never forgot the sense of awe that had pulsed through him. Making love with Carly, he'd felt as if he'd captured a sunbeam in his hands.

That wondrous sense of "something special" hadn't faded. If anything, it felt as if it had been utterly underscored.

His heart racing in his chest, he kissed Carly over

and over again, fanning flames that were, even now, already over the top. Flames that threatened to incinerate them both and reduce them to a single fused, burnt, shriveled crisp.

Ten minutes, Carly realized somewhere at the height of her surrender, ten minutes was all it had taken. Ten minutes from the time Hawk had knocked on her door until she was here like this with him, her body nude and wanting.

Aching.

All it had taken was ten minutes to make her abandon her charade and silently own up to how much she still wanted him.

How much she still yearned for him.

On the floor, with nothing between them but red-hot desire, Carly immersed herself in the sensuality of the world that had temporarily opened up for her. There was almost a frantic sense of urgency to avail herself of all this.

Instinctively she knew that soon, very soon, everything would recede, and she would go back to doing what she had to. Back to being the responsible one. The only one who could rescue her sister from a life of servitude and hell—if not worse.

But for now, for this moment frozen in time, she was just Carly Finn, madly, hopelessly and eternally in love with Hawk Bledsoe, and nothing and no one else mattered outside of this.

Outside of the two of them.

Her body primed, her pulses visibly throbbing, Carly

arched beneath him, silently making him aware that she was ready.

More than ready.

Ready for their union. A union of the body and the soul.

She wondered if he knew that she was his for all eternity. That she was wedded to him until all time ceased, even though words to that effect had never been said over them.

No priest, no minister or justice of the peace could have cemented their union more indelibly.

She was married to him and always would be, no matter what separate directions their two paths in life would ultimately take them. She knew that now.

Once more sealing his mouth to hers, he wove his fingers through hers, and then Hawk thrust himself into her. He was home. It was completed. Their union was reinforced.

And then, after a heartbeat had passed, they began to move in unison, melting into the same dance that they had discovered up in that hayloft so long ago.

The languid tempo stepped up, growing more demanding and urgent with each passing second until the final crescendo found them, sending them crashing over the edge still clinging on to one another, holding on for support, for love.

Slowly, his heartbeat began to slow down until it finally reached a rate that didn't threaten to match the speed of light. And as it slowed, his breathing returned to normal.

Hawk became aware that he held her to him with one

arm wrapped around her, while with his other hand, he gently, slowly, stroked her hair. The ends of it were splayed out along his chest, her head cradled against his rigid pectorals. He could feel her heartbeat mingling with his. Or maybe the two had merged into one.

He found the latter thought comforting.

It was as if the past ten years had never happened. As if his heart hadn't been ripped apart by the callous words she'd uttered.

Words he no longer believed to have been true.

For some reason, she'd lied to him to make him leave town. Why didn't seem important, at least not right now.

It took Hawk more than a couple of minutes to find enough breath to enable him to speak.

The words left his lips slowly, as if languidly coasting on a spring breeze that had yet to come. "Nice to know some things haven't changed."

"What do you mean?"

Too tired to lift her head, Carly asked the question with her cheek still pressed against his chest, unaware that her warm breath was tantalizing his skin with each word she uttered.

"I think that's rather obvious," Hawk answered with a soft laugh. Then because her silence made him think that perhaps it wasn't so obvious to her after all, he said, "You can still reduce me to a palpitating mass of desires, needs and emotions faster than a speeding bullet. I find that pretty impressive."

This time Carly raised her head to look at him. The admission he'd just made left him momentarily vulnerable, exposed, and she knew he was aware of that. If she said something flippant, she'd be protecting herself, but it was a safe bet that it would also succeed in making him pull back, away from her.

Because he was vulnerable, she didn't want to hurt him, didn't want to make him feel that he was the only one in this relationship who felt that way. The only one who was exposed.

So she smiled at him, allowing the sentiment she felt to reach her eyes as she said, "Right back at you, Hawk." And then she took a breath before adding, "But this really doesn't change anything."

He wasn't so sure about that, but he knew better than to say so at a time like this. "We'll talk." The word "later" was an unspoken given.

Before she could even think to challenge his assumption, Hawk surprised her by shifting. With his hands on her waist, he deftly moved her so that she was now over him.

It was hard to carry on any sort of a serious argument with their more than warm bodies pressed against one another like this.

She let him win the round.

For now.

Because in doing so, she won, as well.

And winning, as they said, was everything. As long as it was with Hawk.

Chapter 8

So much for staying strong, Carly upbraided herself as she slowly descended back to reality and the demands of the world around her.

Now what?

Although she was incredibly aware of the man lying beside her, that didn't change the situation. They couldn't actually progress anywhere from here. The earth might have stood still and caught on fire when they made love just now, but that didn't block out the years gone by or even start a new chapter in their lives.

What had just transpired between them, she supposed, could be thought of as an aberration at best. A single aberration.

"So," she finally said, unable to take the silence anymore, "same time, same place ten years from now?" She was doing her damndest to sound chipper and not like a woman who expected promises.

Hawk turned to look at her. "Don't," he chided. His face appeared as if it was carved out of stone.

"Don't what?"

"Don't do that."

Same old Hawk, she thought. No one could ever accuse this man of running off at the mouth. There were times when he doled out words as if each one came from a rare collection.

"Don't do what?" Carly pressed a little more sharply.

"Don't be flippant."

Well, she couldn't deny she was guilty of that, but it wasn't because she was being cynical. She was just behaving the way she thought he'd want her to. Like the women he was probably accustomed to encountering— both in and out of bed.

"Okay," she said gamely, "what would you like me to be?"

His eyes held hers for a moment before he said, "Honest."

Was he accusing her of lying? About what? He couldn't possibly be referring to their last conversation ten years ago, so what was he talking about?

"I'm always honest," she fired back defensively, then prayed he wouldn't delve too deeply in order to point out the contradiction.

The expression on his face when she said that told her that he knew better—or that he thought he did.

But he didn't take her to task for the lie she'd just uttered or challenge the words she'd told him ten years ago that had sent him packing and on his way—the words she'd used to tell him that she didn't love him. He knew Carly well enough to know that she could have never made love with him, especially like that, if love wasn't at least a factor.

"Carly, I want you to tell me the truth," he began.

Carly headed him off, teasingly saying the words that she'd heard many a man wanted to have the woman he'd just bedded say. "Yes, the earth moved."

Hawk didn't laugh the way she'd hoped he would. His subject was too serious for him to laugh.

"That's not what I'm asking you," he replied evenly.

Nerves began to dance throughout her body again. Hawk had always seen right through her, except for that one time. Her words had hurt him too much for him to see beyond the pain, to guess why she was saying what she had.

But now he seemed deadly serious, and his eyes felt as if they were boring into her very soul, lifting words, reading thoughts.

Wanting to momentarily escape, she started to rise. Before she could stand up, his fingers tightened around her wrist.

She wasn't going anywhere.

"I thought you had murders to investigate," Carly reminded him.

That was the whole point, didn't she see that? "I do, and I don't want you to wind up joining that unholy number."

Was it that he actually cared about her, or that she

represented extra paperwork? *Don't get carried away, remember? No future, you know that.*

She waved away his voiced concern. "I'm fine. In case you weren't paying attention, I'm alive and well."

"I was paying very close attention," he assured her. "And for the record, I want to keep you that way—'alive and well.'"

Hawk really did need to lighten up. She relaxed a little as she asked, "What makes you think anything is going to change?"

That was a safe bet. Her remaining safe was not. He had a feeling that Grayson might already see through her act—because what else could it really be? Carly was way too intelligent, too savvy to be taken in by a second-rate motivational speaker no matter how slick he tried to be.

She'd had him going at first, Hawk thought, but he saw through it now. Because she really *was* still Carly, for all her protests to the contrary.

"That's simple enough," he told her, then warned, "Grayson doesn't like being played."

"Who's playing Grayson?" she asked innocently.

Hawk didn't buy the act for a second and rather resented that she was continuing with this charade after they'd made love. She was definitely not being honest with him.

"You are," he bit off. When she opened her mouth to protest, he ordered curtly, "Save it. You're still the same woman you were ten years ago. *That* woman wasn't a fool."

"I don't know about that," she murmured under her

breath, remembering the way she'd ached, sending him away. Maybe she shouldn't have.

Granted he was more successful now, but he didn't look any happier than he had back then. As a matter of fact, he looked less so, and she certainly wasn't ready to do cartwheels over the course her life had taken. She was still struggling to make a go of the farm, or had been before she'd decided to walk away from it and Cold Plains. That plan had involved being determined to start over somewhere else.

But she wanted to start over not just for herself but her sister, as well, something that was proving impossible to do since Mia wanted to remain here to become the Bride of Dracula—or at least his first lieutenant.

"She wasn't a fool," he repeated. "She was noble, loyal and giving. And she was the type to make sacrifices."

He knew, she thought as she looked into his eyes. Hawk knew. Knew what she'd done all those years ago, knew what it had cost her. But until she confirmed it, he had only his speculation to go on. "You're giving me too much credit," she said dismissively.

Lying there, he began to stroke her thigh as he spoke. "And you're not giving me enough. I want you out of here, Carly. Grayson is trouble. He has blood on his hands, and despite the wide, artificial grin on his face, he wouldn't hesitate to eliminate whoever gets in his way—male or female." Hawk's meaning was very clear.

For a moment, she thought about continuing her act. But then she decided not to keep up the pretense, which meant trying to defend Grayson's character and actions.

She wasn't *that* good an actress. She loathed the man and what Hawk was saying really scared her. Not that she was afraid for herself—she could take care of herself—but she was exceedingly worried about her sister. Mia was apparently an integral part of Grayson's plans for the future.

"I can't leave Mia," she told him flatly, thinking that was the end of the discussion.

Hawk surprised her by saying, "I know how you feel, but Mia's a big girl, she can look out for herself."

She'd forgotten that in his case, his sense of family left something to be desired.

"No, she can't," Carly insisted. "If I don't do something, Mia's going to get married in two weeks to a man she doesn't love. A man who's too old for her. A man whose first wife went mysteriously missing. I don't want the same thing happening to Mia, not when I can stop it."

She was *finally* being honest, he thought. Took her long enough. "So I was right."

That caught her up short. "Most likely," she allowed, "but about what?"

"That you're still in Cold Plains for a reason. That you're not hanging around because Grayson charmed you into remaining." His mouth curved for the first time, his smile stirring her the way it always did. "I knew you weren't that empty-headed."

Carly laughed shortly. "Still have that silver tongue, I see."

He knew she was taking exception to the word *empty-headed,* but he made no attempt to apologize because that had been his concern, that she'd somehow lost all her common sense and that almost seemed inconceivable.

"You could always think for yourself," he continued, "not follow the crowd like some lemming, programmed to drop off the edge of a cliff straight into the ocean."

In all honesty, she hadn't wanted him to think that she was captivated by Grayson. That was just too demeaning. "So you understand that I have to stay until I can get her to see reason—or until I can find a way to kidnap the bride before the wedding? At this point," she confessed, "I don't care which way I do it as long as I can keep Mia from marrying that man."

He wondered if she'd thought through the consequences or, if she had, if she was turning a blind eye toward them. "If you wind up having to kidnap her, she's going to hate you."

Carly shrugged. Mia already blamed her for what she considered her unhappy, deprived life. "Won't be the first time."

Hawk sighed. He might have known trying to talk her out of it was useless. "So you're not going to listen to me and get out of Cold Plains?"

"I'll get out of Cold Plains—after I have Mia," she assured him. "Not before."

They were lying here, carrying on a conversation, dressed in nothing but the warmth of their own body heat. Body heat that reached out to the other.

Hawk slipped his arm around her and drew closer to her. He propped himself up on his elbow and looked down into her face. "Were you always this stubborn?" he asked her.

"Always," she whispered.

Hawk shook his head. "Funny, I don't seem to remember that."

"What do you remember?" she asked.

The smile that came over Hawk's features told her exactly what he remembered. The same thing she did. The lovemaking that nurtured their souls and kept them both sane, making their stark world bearable.

Rather than say anything, Hawk showed her.

He stayed the night, even though when he'd first stopped on her doorstep, he'd had every intention of returning to his hotel room at the end of the evening. Somehow, he just never made it out of the room.

When Hawk finally woke up the next morning, he reached for her.

And found only emptiness beside him.

Carly was gone.

He was programmed to think the worst in any given situation, and all traces of sleep and contentment instantly fled. He was alert and ready to go searching for Carly.

But the next moment, the scent of freshly brewed coffee mingling with the tempting smell of bacon and eggs frying registered. He sincerely doubted Grayson or any of the man's robotlike minions were here, making him breakfast.

Pausing only to pull on his jeans, Hawk padded down to the kitchen in his bare feet.

He was relieved to find Carly there, standing over the stove, making breakfast. Instead of wearing her own clothes, she had on the light blue shirt he'd worn last night. It hung down to her knees, and he had the feeling that she was completely naked underneath.

He had difficulty reining in his imagination. The sight of Carly like that made him ache for her all over again.

Moving quietly as he'd been trained to do, Hawk came up behind the woman who had rocked his world last night, rocked it the way it hadn't been, even remotely, these past ten years.

He stood behind her and slipped his arms around her waist. He felt her stiffen as she grabbed for another skillet, her hand wrapping around the handle as if she intended to use it as a weapon.

"Down, tiger, it's only me," he whispered against her ear, managing to all but singe her very skin with his warm breath.

Carly breathed a sigh of relief. She released her grip on the skillet, leaving it on the back, dormant burner.

"There is no 'only' when it comes to you," she informed him. Then before he could explore her comment, she told him to "Sit down, breakfast is almost ready."

Pulling over the two plates she'd set out on the counter, Carly began to divide up the eggs and bacon. She topped it off with the toast that she'd just finished buttering.

She then set the pan down and gave Hawk the larger portion. As she remembered, he always had an appetite first thing in the morning. Conversely, hers always took a couple of hours to kick in.

"By the way," she said as she set his plate before him, "some FBI agent you are. You didn't even stir when I slipped out of bed this morning. I thought you guys are supposed to sleep with one eye open."

He took the fresh coffee she'd just poured for him. It was as black as he imagined Grayson's heart was. For a second, he savored the heat that rose up from the cup before taking a deep, life-affirming sip.

"You completely wore me out," he said matter-of-factly, then added, "I'll have to work on that."

Was that last part just an off-the-cuff remark, or did he mean something by it, she wondered. "Working on it" made it sound as if she would be there to see if he succeeded.

Don't read anything into it, she warned herself. This was nice, being here like this with him, but it too was an aberration. The man was here for a reason, and she wasn't it. He had a job to do, and then he would be on his way.

She had to remember that, Carly silently insisted. Otherwise, she left herself open to devastation. She couldn't go through that twice, loving him and watching him walking away from her. She wouldn't survive a second time—if she allowed herself to love him again.

So this time, it's going to be just fun, no strings.

"You haven't lost your touch," Hawk said after taking a hearty bite of his breakfast. He looked at her for a long moment, then added, "Not with anything."

She could feel warmth creeping up the sides of her

neck, reaching her face. Any second now, she would turn a really embarrassing shade of pink, she thought, upset with her inability to bank down feelings.

"So what's the plan?" she asked abruptly, trying to change the subject. Hawk was exceedingly focused, so if she could just get him to think about his reasons for being here, she thought it was a safe bet that she could turn lime-green and he wouldn't notice. At least not immediately.

"With Grayson," she added, in case he thought she was asking about their future together.

She already knew the answer to that one. They had no future together. She'd taken care of that when she'd initially sent him on his way. This was just a lovely, quick trip down memory lane, but she wasn't going to make herself crazy by thinking that maybe they were getting a second chance to do it right this time.

They were both too far along on their separate paths for her to think that life offered any kind of "do-overs." It didn't. One had to live with the consequences of one's actions, and she was prepared to do just that, even if it felt as if she were swallowing razor blades.

"The plan is that I continue rattling cages, asking questions, trying to get someone to testify against Grayson and to hopefully give us the missing evidence that ties that bastard to the five murders. I know in my gut he did it—or ordered it done—but I can't prove it.

"So far, the guy's been a slick devil. We've connected the women to Cold Plains, but we haven't been able to connect them to Grayson—yet." He thought of Micah and wondered again where the man was. Grayson's twin still wasn't answering his phone, but he refused to think that Micah was dead. Men like him brought death to people; they weren't mowed down by it.

If he could just get a hold of Micah and ask him some key questions, maybe things would clear up a little.

At any rate, it was something he was going to look into—as soon as he finished breakfast. Granted he was indulging himself, but he rarely did that, and who knew when he could get a home-cooked meal again?

"Everything okay?" Carly asked as she sat down on the stool next to his at the counter.

"The meal's fantastic," he said in a tone that told her he was leaving out more than he was saying.

Fork raised, she forgot about eating for a moment. Leaning her head against her hand, she looked at him.

"So what isn't okay?" she asked.

What wasn't okay was that he suddenly had her to worry about. She wasn't one of those women who stood off to the side, observing or waiting to be rescued. She was the kind of woman who charged out and took matters into her own hands. She was the kind of woman who made him worry and kept him up at night. Knowing the answer he was going to get, he gave it a shot, anyway. "Any way I can convince you to leave dealing with Grayson up to me?"

She smiled and shook her head. "Not even a repeat performance of last night," she answered. There might have been a smile on her lips, but her eyes, he noted, were very serious as she added, "I take care of my own, Hawk, you know that. And Mia's my sister, that makes her my problem."

"She's old enough to make her own decisions," he pointed out again.

"Only if she makes the right ones," was Carly's good-humored albeit stubborn response.

It was futile to argue with her. She would only succeed in getting him to lose his temper.

Same old Carly, he couldn't help thinking.

Despite his concern, Hawk caught himself grinning for the remainder of their time together. It was way too late for them after all these years had gone by—but that didn't mean that he couldn't savor the small moment that had unexpectedly been carved out for them at this junction.

He could.

And he would.

Chapter 9

After breakfast, just before he and Carly went their separate ways that morning, Hawk decided to try one last time to talk a little sense into Carly, to no avail.

She listened quietly as Hawk continued to enumerate all the reasons—again—why what she was doing was tantamount to juggling with loaded pistols. When he was finished, he could tell by the expression on her face that he had made no headway whatsoever in making her come around to his way of thinking.

Instead, rather than arguing with him, she pointed out the upside of having her continue to pose as one of the faithful in Grayson's circle.

"Think of it this way, Hawk. You need to have a person on the inside to be your eyes and ears. I'll be that person."

That was all well and good, if she were a trained special agent—and someone else. But she wasn't trained in undercover work, and she was Carly, someone he didn't want taking any risks.

So he shook his head and got ready to leave. He looked down into her eyes one last time. "I don't want to see anything happening to you."

Carly smiled at his concern. She wouldn't have been able to explain why, but the very fact that he was worried made her feel safe.

"That makes two of us," she assured Hawk. "Don't worry, I'll be careful."

He really wished he could believe her, Hawk thought, walking over to where he had left his car last night. But where her sister was involved, Carly would take whatever risks she felt were necessary in order to save Mia.

Getting into his vehicle, Hawk blew out a long breath. The best way to protect Carly at this point was to nail Grayson as quickly as possible for at least one of the murders. Once he had that, once he could point to Grayson's connection to one murder, he had a feeling the rest would fall into place.

Preoccupied, he inserted his key into the ignition. Just as he was about to start the car, he saw that there was a folded piece of paper on his dashboard.

Staring at it, Hawk frowned.

He was positive that hadn't been there last night when he drove up to Carly's house. His hand automatically covered the hilt of his service revolver as he looked around slowly, deliberately. But other than Carly's house, the barn and the corral, nothing was visible for miles. Whoever had broken into his vehicle and left the paper on his dashboard was long gone.

Not knowing what to expect, he took out his handkerchief, and holding it by the edge, he opened the folded paper and read:

"Please meet me at the Hanging Tree at 10 this morning. I urgently need to speak with you. Come alone."

That was it. Three terse sentences. No signature, no indication what this was about. For all he knew, he was being set up.

But this could also be on the level. It might be one of Grayson's people who'd had enough, was unable to break away and was willing to trade information for help in getting out of the cult—because at this point, that was what it was. A cult.

Hawk glanced at his watch. The note said to be there by ten. Because he'd lingered over breakfast—and over Carly—he didn't have all that much time to spare. The reference to the meeting place made him think that perhaps he was dealing with someone who was a native of the area. Outsiders didn't know about the oak tree's nickname.

The Hanging Tree had gotten its name because of a story that had made the rounds over a hundred years ago. The biggest branch on it was uniquely bent and actually pointed down. The story had it that an outlaw gang caught the sheriff who had been pursuing them, and that they hung him from the biggest, strongest branch of this massive tree and then just rode away, leaving the sheriff to die. The branch miraculous bent down far enough for him to reach the ground with his feet. Freeing himself, he went on to track down and avenge himself of each of the outlaws who had left him to die.

When he was a kid, Hawk liked to pretend he was that sheriff, hunting down outlaws and dispensing his own brand of justice. After a while, the lines between reality and make-believe blurred a little. He supposed that story had gotten him thinking about becoming a law-enforcement agent.

Before he took off for the appointed meeting place, Hawk called Rosenbloom at the cabin. "I just wanted you to know where I'm going in case I don't get back."

"You want backup?" Rosenbloom asked.

The agent sounded eager to get out of the cabin. Hawk couldn't blame him. But he also couldn't use him right now. "The note said to come alone."

He could almost *hear* Rosenbloom's frown over the phone. "Since when do you listen to notes?"

Since I don't want to jeopardize this case, I'm in a hurry to wrap it up and keep Carly safe, because the woman doesn't have enough sense to stay the hell out of this.

"I didn't call you to argue," he told the other man. "I just want you to know where I'm going."

"Got it."

Hawk hung up and drove straight to the appointed place. Taking precautions, he got out of the vehicle and slowly circled around. The man he saw standing by the tree and impatiently shifting from one foot to the other was a stranger to him.

But as he drew closer, Hawk realized that this was someone he'd seen recently. But where? And with whom?

Was it a setup? Hawk wondered again. Whoever this guy was, he definitely appeared uneasy. Why? Because he was afraid of being watched? Or because he was afraid he might get cut down in the cross fire?

Dr. Rafe Black looked at his watch. It was three minutes past ten.

Where the hell was Bledsoe, anyway?

He dragged a hand through his black hair. Three months ago, he had been blissfully unaware that Cold Plains, Wyoming, even existed. And then he'd received a phone call from a woman he'd been involved with a little more than nine months ago for exactly one night. At first, when she told him her name, he couldn't even place her.

And then he remembered. She was a sweet-faced, almost timid young woman.

Abby Michaels had tracked him down and was calling because she thought he should know that he was now the father of a newborn, healthy baby boy named Devin.

Stunned by the news, he took a moment to recover. When he began firing questions at Abby, the line went dead. He tried to shrug it off as a practical joke that one of his colleagues was playing on him, but he had the uneasy feeling that it wasn't.

And he was right.

A week later, he received a brown envelope with a photograph of a male infant. It could have been his own photograph taken at that age. The child had the same dark eyes, the same dark hair that he'd had. In addition, the baby had his mother's nose and small, rosebud mouth. One look, and he *knew* this was his child—and Abby's.

A letter was included with the photograph. In it, Abby asked him for ten thousand dollars to help care for the baby, instructing that it be wired to a bank in Laramie.

He did as she asked, going down to Laramie with the hopes of finding Abby, his son and some answers. However, none of it materialized. Abby and the baby were nowhere to be found. Wondering if he'd been duped, Rafe nonetheless seriously considered hiring a private investigator to track down Abby and his son.

He was still debating that course of action when he saw the news story about the five murdered women being found in different locations. In all honesty, after a long day at the hospital, he was only half paying attention when he saw Abby's photo being flashed on the screen. That got his attention immediately. She was one of the dead women.

Rafe had tuned in just in time to hear that all five women, including a Jane Doe, had Cold Plains, Wyoming, in common. He started packing immediately.

Cold Plains was where the answers were. Once he arrived, he went about the business of opening up a practice, thinking it would help him blend in. He was hoping to pick up enough information to enable him to locate his son. After all, people told their doctor things they didn't share with their friends or families. Maybe he would hear something useful that would help.

He'd hardly been in Cold Plains more than two weeks when he heard that there was an FBI special agent in town looking into the deaths of these women. Into Abby's death.

Confident that this was the break he'd been looking for, Rafe had decided to contact Special Agent Bledsoe and share what he knew about Abby. However, Rafe instinctively understood the need for caution and secrecy. Apparently, there was a killer loose, and he didn't want to attract undue attention, which might result in his son being harmed—if the boy was actually here, something he hadn't established yet.

"Who are you?" A deep, low voice behind him growled out the question.

Caught completely by surprise, Rafe spun around, not knowing what to expect and wishing he'd brought some kind of weapon with him. Half braced to be staring into the face of a killer, Rafe exhaled a loud sigh of relief when he saw that the man facing him was the FBI special agent he was waiting for.

"Damn, but you scared me," Rafe told him, his hand splayed across his chest.

Hawk made no apologies. "Didn't know if I was walking into a trap."

Seeing the ironic humor in the situation, Rafe laughed shortly. "That makes two of us." He put out his hand to the special agent. "I'm Dr. Black. Rafe Black," he added.

After a beat, Hawk took the offered hand and returned the handshake.

He glanced over his shoulder at the Hanging Tree. "Well, Dr. Black, I can't say that this is exactly a typical meeting place. Why did you want to meet me out here and not in your office?" Hawk asked.

That, at least, was a simple question to answer. "Because I didn't want anyone overhearing what I had to tell you."

Hawk was still waiting to find out what this was all about and if it in any way helped to shed some light on the murders he was investigating. "Which is?"

Rafe took a deep breath and then plunged into his story. "I had a relationship with one of the murdered women, Abby Michaels."

His interest piqued, Hawk continued to scan the area, making sure that they weren't caught by surprise. So far, they appeared to be alone out here.

"Go on."

Rafe backtracked a little. "Well, not so much a relationship as a one-night stand."

Hawk did his best not to sound impatient, but it wasn't easy. The level of his adrenaline was rising. "Which is it?"

"A one-night stand," Rafe said definitively. "At least I thought that was all it was. But three months ago, I got a phone call from Abby saying that she'd just given birth to a baby boy and I was the baby's father."

Hawk looked at him sharply. This was the first he'd heard about a baby. Would they find yet another, much smaller body somewhere out there? "Did the numbers work out?"

"Yeah, that's about the time we hooked up. Abby sent me a photograph of my son." He took it out of the pocket of his jacket and glanced at it before holding it up for the special agent. "This could have been a picture of me as a newborn."

Hawk took the photograph and studied it for a moment before handing it back to the doctor. "You are aware that most babies look alike."

Rafe knew what the agent was implying, but he was convinced that this was his son. And just as convinced that he had to find him somehow.

"No, this one's mine," he said with conviction. Then because the agent was looking at him a bit skeptically, he added, "It's a gut feeling. I *know* he's mine, Bledsoe," he told Hawk.

"I'm the last one to dismiss a gut feeling," Hawk assured him. A gut feeling was what had gotten him this far. Granted it was by no means an exact science, but he'd found that his instincts were right over seventy percent of the time. "Why are you telling me this?" he asked.

"Because I need your help," Rafe said without any fanfare. "I can't find him. I came as soon as I saw the story on TV about the murdered women all being from Cold Plains. I thought maybe she'd left my son with her relatives, but I'm beginning to think that maybe she didn't even come back here between the time she called me and the time she was killed. I've been asking around if anyone's heard anything about a motherless baby somewhere in the area, but so far, nobody seems to know anything. Or," he amended, "if they know, they're not saying."

"Yeah, I get that a lot," Hawk told him with a dismissive laugh that had no humor to it. "Did you go to the police chief with your story?" he asked out of curiosity. Fargo definitely wouldn't have been his first choice, but then maybe the man was different with the people of his town.

"Yes, I did." Rafe's frown told him just how far that had gotten him. His next words confirmed it. "Man's not very friendly," Rafe testified. "Said he hadn't heard anything about any of the women in his 'community' having any unwanted children, but I get the feeling that he's not telling me the truth."

Welcome to the club, Hawk thought. "I'll keep my eyes open and let you know if I find out anything," he promised the doctor. In exchange he was hoping the doctor would do the same. "Listen, since you got me out here, maybe you can answer a question for me."

Was it his imagination, or did the doctor look a little apprehensive before finally saying, "Sure, if I can."

Hawk's question concerned the newly constructed clinic that Grayson had had built according to his specifications. For a medical clinic, it was exceedingly cold, sterile and unwelcoming.

"I noticed that the town now has this Urgent Care Center that Grayson was responsible for building." When he'd left town initially, any medical care had to be sought outside the town, over in a neighboring county. "I'm picking up things that don't seem right to me."

Rafe knew exactly what the special agent was referring to. He'd become aware of strange practices himself, practices that went against the norm. He'd also noticed that he hadn't been asked to join the care center. Was that because he was new to the town, or was it because of some other reason? Such as, if he knew exactly what was going on behind closed doors, he would request an investigation?

"By that, you mean like the fact that people aren't allowed to leave the facility until they get a complete, clean bill of health from the attending physician—even if they have ongoing conditions such as diabetes or heart trouble?" Rafe asked.

Hawk nodded his head. "That's what I mean." What had gotten his attention in the first place was finding out about the unorthodox case he was now recounting. "I talked to someone the other day who said that her cousin accidentally hit his head on the pavement, so he went to the Center to get some stitches—and he hasn't been heard from since. This cousin also has a heart murmur, according to the woman I talked with."

Rafe nodded. That didn't surprise him. "Sounds about right. People who have started coming to me looking for treatment are people who don't want to have anything to do with the care center. Margaret Chase—" he brought up the name of one of the town's oldest residents "—told me that some of her friends have gone missing, and the last time she'd heard from one of the women, she was going in to the clinic to get treatment for a persistent cough that just wouldn't go away."

He'd already noted that the people he'd seen around town who belonged to Grayson's dedicated followers all seemed to be robust, healthy-looking specimens of humanity. Now that he thought more about it, he couldn't remember hearing anyone even coughing or sneezing. No one seemed to have so much as a hangnail. Everyone seemed to be the flourishing picture of health.

Was that by design?

Where were all the sick people, the ones with disabilities? For that matter, where were the homely ones? The ones who were not perfect?

This was beginning to sound eerily gruesome, Hawk thought.

For all he knew, Grayson might actually be trying to fashion some perfect society filled with movie-star-handsome men, women and children.

And Carly was right in the thick of it, he thought suddenly.

Damn but he needed to get her to back away from all this for her own good. Maybe if he swore to her that he would rescue Mia the first chance he got, he could get her to listen to him and leave Cold Plains before Grayson found out what Carly was up to and things became really ugly.

But even as he thought it, Hawk knew that there was no reasoning with Carly, not once she made up her mind. There'd been a time when he'd admired her strong will and strength of character, but right now, it could be the very quality that could get her killed. He had no illusions about Grayson, not after he'd reread the report on the man's background.

"Look, Doc," he proposed out of the blue, "if I promise to keep my ears and eyes open for any information about an orphaned newborn, will you see what you can find out about what's happening to those people in the Urgent Care Center? I mean, it's not like a circus clown car when dozens of people go in and then don't come back out again." Rosenbloom had compiled a list of people who had gone into the care center in the past six months but hadn't been seen or heard from afterward.

So where were they? Had they been asked to leave town or, he thought darkly, were they merely eliminated if they didn't cooperate? It sounded almost absurd. He could easily see Grayson justifying this action because he wanted to purify the strain, form a society of healthy, pretty people.

The man wasn't a charming hypnotist, he was a crass, manipulative bastard, and the sooner he could take Grayson down, the better.

It was a thought he hung on to as he drove back to the cabin. He needed to fill his team in on this newest twist, and it was done better in person.

Chapter 10

Depositing the three, extra-large containers of dark roast coffee on the table, Hawk looked at the three men who gave every indication of having severe cases of cabin fever. "How are we doing with our Jane Doe? Any progress finding out who she really was?"

Rosenbloom pried the lid off his giant container and took a long swig of the still-hot coffee before giving him an answer. Only after the black liquid had wound its way through his system did he frown critically at his container.

"What did they use to make this, trail mix?" he asked.

"I guess gourmet coffee hasn't made an appearance in Cold Plains yet," Jeffers quipped, seemingly grateful to have something black and hot to sustain him.

"Hey, it's better than nothing," Patterson commented, downing all but the last third of his container.

"Jane Doe?" Hawk prodded, looking from one man to the next. All three shook their heads.

And then Jeffers put it into words. "We haven't found any missing persons report matching her description so far. At least not in Wyoming in the last four years. I'm going to check the out-of-state reports next." His expression said he didn't hold out too much hope. "But after four years, this seems like a pretty cold case."

That wasn't what he wanted to hear. "Well, then, warm it up," Hawk instructed.

Rosenbloom turned his chair back to face the laptop on his side of the table. "By the way, how's life in the outside world?" he asked. "The sky still blue?"

"Do people still get to listen to the news?" Patterson put in.

Hawk ignored the flippant remarks and filled the men in on his meeting with the new doctor and the latter's hunt for his missing son. He went on to tell them about the physician's theory about what he believed was going on in the Urgent Care Clinic.

Jeffers ate up every word. "You know, once we wind this up, we've got the makings of one hell of a movie script here," he commented.

Hawk laughed shortly and shook his head. "Yeah, if we ever *do* wrap this up." Right now, he had his doubts about that happening. There was no denying that Grayson was slick. Nothing seemed to stick to the man. And without the information that Micah was supposed to provide, who knew if they would ever be able to pin anything on the so-called community leader.

"Do I detect a lack of faith?" Jeffers asked with a touch of surprise.

It wasn't so much a lack of faith at play here as a healthy respect for the reality of the situation. On the average, more cases remained open than were closed. "It's just that everywhere we turn for answers, all we find are more questions."

"Well, my money's on us," Jeffers said cheerfully. "Don't forget, we're the good guys," he reminded his superior.

"Yeah, well, if we don't get out of this cabin soon, we'll be too stiff and out of shape to do anybody any good," Rosenbloom complained. He was far from happy about being confined this way.

Patterson's nerves were getting frayed. "Maybe if you started cooking something that wasn't exclusively made up of fat, salt and sugar, we wouldn't be *getting* out of shape."

He had to nip this before it got out of hand. Ordinarily, the three men worked well together, but that was when they weren't living in one another's pockets 24/7. "You three keep this up, and I'm going to have to send you to your rooms without your supper," Hawk warned, looking from one to the other.

He got his point across. They were bickering like children. Not that he didn't secretly sympathize with them. Staying in the cabin for an indefinite amount of time, waiting to finally be able to spring into action, could drive anyone crazy. But playing the waiting game was all part of the job. Not a pleasant part, but a part nonetheless.

The moment Hawk started toward the door, Rosenbloom was instantly alert. "Where are you going?" he asked.

"It's time to see if I can rattle the head honcho's cage and hopefully get him to make a mistake." Hawk paused by the door just before leaving. "If I'm not back by tomorrow, pick him up for questioning," he told Rosenbloom.

"You think he'd actually try something?" Jeffers asked.

"He does know you're an FBI agent, right?" Patterson asked.

"He does, but desperate men resort to desperate measures. Especially if they think they can get away with it."

He had no illusions about Grayson. If he had had those women murdered, then what was another body more or less? At this stage, having gotten away with so much, Grayson had probably developed a god complex, he reasoned. Or at the very least, thought he was invulnerable.

So far, he was right.

"Remember, one day," Hawk reminded his men as he went out. The way he saw it, it was always better to be safe than sorry.

Rather than corner Grayson alone in his office and ask him questions that the man was probably going to respond to with lies, Hawk decided to observe the man in his full glory first. He wanted to see for himself exactly what all the excitement was about.

Hawk was aware of several motivational speakers who had managed to do very well for themselves, building up an empire based on books, audio tapes and speaking engagement fees. He'd heard that Grayson had had a modest amount of success following that route, but obviously the man wasn't strictly interested in making a living or even in the "calling" of helping people fulfill their true potential, something that was the supposed cornerstone of every motivational speaker's philosophy.

The only one Samuel Grayson wanted to help was Samuel Grayson, and apparently the way he did it, at least in part, was to boost his ego by seeing just how many people he could get to pledge their undying loyalty to him.

As he stood in the back of the room, near the door he'd used to slip into the auditorium, Hawk watched Grayson become a dynamo of barely harnessed energy. Moving about the entire stage and remaining in perpetual motion, Grayson created the illusion of addressing each person in the room individually. He singled them out, as if that particular person was the only one who mattered at that particular time.

It was a pretty neat parlor trick, Hawk couldn't help thinking. Admittedly, it was a skill that not that many people had.

What was the man's end game? he wondered. Was Grayson just doing this to see how many people he could get under his thumb, vowing to follow him to the ends of the earth—and beyond? Or did he have almost a *physical* need for all this adulation? Was he stirring everyone up for a reason, for some personal gain at the end of the line, or was it all just a power trip?

Most of all, how had he benefited—if he actually had—from the deaths of those five women? Why *those* particular women? And were they the only dead bodies to be found, or were there more that they just hadn't come across yet?

Hawk had an uneasy feeling it was the latter, but for now, he shut the thought away and observed Grayson in his element.

"You can't let life drag you down," Grayson said, his words and gaze taking in each and every person seated at the seminar. His voice swelled as he asked, "What do we do with negative thoughts?"

"We flush them away," the audience chanted in response.

Grayson cupped his ear as if trying to make out a faint sound. "I can't hear you," he announced in a singsong voice.

The audience responded with enthusiasm, repeating what they'd said, only louder this time. However, it still wasn't loud enough to suit Grayson. He kept egging them on to say the phrase louder and louder until they were all shouting the words.

Only then did he smile with approval, an approval his audience ate up and reveled in, like children allowed to temporarily sit at the adult table.

The guy's a real puppet master, Hawk thought, his eyes sweeping over the faces of the audience that he was able to see from where he stood. They looked as if they were in the throes of rapture. It reminded him of a black-and-white film clip he'd seen on one of the history channels, chronicling a dictator's rise to power just before the fateful second world war.

A chill went down his spine.

Hawk saw no difference between the dictator and Grayson. Both appeared enamored with the sound of their own voices. And with the desire to seize power through the people they so obviously commanded.

It was enough to make a man sick.

As Grayson moved about the raised platform he'd had specially built according to his exact specifications, focused on working up his audience the way he did every day as he brought each of his seminars to a close, his eyes met Hawk's.

Hawk was immediately alert. There was no quizzical pause, no indication that Grayson didn't know who he was looking at. Instead, there was an evident smugness, as if he was well pleased with his performance and satisfied that he had created the impression Grayson wanted him to witness.

"That's all for tonight," Grayson finally announced. Taking a hand towel from the podium, he wiped the perspiration from his brow. "I want you all to go to your homes and think about how you can improve upon what you're doing and how you can enrich your neighbors' lives through your own evolvement."

Yeah, and how to put more money into your fearless leader's pockets, I'll bet, Hawk thought cynically. Grayson was as phony as a three-dollar bill. If he hadn't believed it before, he did now. What completely mystified him was how nobody seemed to be able to see through the other man's facade. It was all sparkling glitter and hyped-up rhetoric.

As the meeting broke up, Hawk watched the people in Grayson's audience rise to their feet, applauding wildly. Those who *didn't* swarm around the speaker began to file out of the auditorium.

A few hung back, neither trying to gain Grayson's attention nor leaving just yet.

He realized that Carly was in that third group. Why was she lingering?

And then he had his explanation. A girl who looked vaguely familiar—was that really Mia, all grown up now?—was part of the circle clustering around Grayson. They all appeared to be eagerly vying for the favor of the speaker's momentary attention.

Carly's sister smiled broadly as he heard Grayson say, "Mia, I need a word with you, please."

"Of course, Samuel," the young woman replied.

She sounded just like a robot, Hawk couldn't help thinking.

Despite the fact that there was half a room between them, his eyes met Carly's and he could see she was thinking the same thing. And that it really upset her. Small wonder.

Grayson, with his lofty seminars and flattering words, with his attention, which made the members of his circle feel as if they were being singled out by God, had managed to brainwash a room full of easily manipulated people, young and old.

To what end? Hawk wondered again.

Was it just to feed his ego, or was there some darker purpose in all this? A dark purpose he wasn't seeing just yet.

He could see why Carly was worried. Hell, he'd been worried himself before he realized that Carly was only putting on a show for Grayson's benefit.

And it was a pretty damn convincing show at that, he thought now, watching her. Though it took some restraint, Hawk made no effort to approach her. As far as he knew, Grayson wasn't aware that he and Carly had a history, and he wanted to keep it that way. Not knowing that little fact would keep Carly a lot safer at the moment. He didn't want to think what might happen if Grayson suspected she had a connection to an FBI special agent—no matter how innocent that connection might actually be.

He watched as Grayson took both of Mia's hands in his. "The ladies have selected a wedding dress for you," he informed her. "You need to make yourself available for a fitting." He bestowed a benevolent smile on the young woman whose hands he still held. "You wouldn't want to offend your husband by not appearing perfect at the ceremony."

"Oh no, Samuel, I would never do that," Mia assured him with immense feeling in her voice.

His voice was patronizing as he said, "That's my girl."

Hawk stole a covert glance at Carly. That was the kind of remark that would have had her seeing red in the old days. Seeing red and putting someone like Grayson in his place.

But she looked perfectly serene now, as if the man's smarmy remark made absolutely no impression whatsoever.

She really was one hell of an actress, Hawk thought again, silently tipping his hat to her. This was a side of Carly that he'd never seen before, hadn't even suspected existed. All he knew was that there was a time when she would have instantly made her feelings about Grayson's crass assumption known.

Hell, she might have even contemplated gutting the man—or making him think that she would.

Hawk suppressed an amused smile. The next moment, he saw that Grayson's eyes had shifted in his direction. Hawk was instantly on his guard.

Walking over to him, hands outstretched as if he were greeting a long-lost brother, Grayson asked in a booming voice, "Am I in the presence of a new convert?" he asked.

Rather than tender a negative answer to the question, Hawk identified himself instead. Taking out his wallet, he opened it to display his ID and held it up for Grayson's perusal.

"I'm special agent Hawk Bledsoe with—"

"The FBI," Grayson concluded with a nod of his head, which seemed more of a dismissal. "Yes, I am well aware what makes you so special, Agent Bledsoe," Grayson replied in a humoring tone that Hawk found exceedingly grating. "To what do I owe this pleasure?" he asked, his tone neutral, giving nothing away.

How much did the man actually know, and how much was he bluffing? Hawk caught himself wondering.

Out loud, he announced, "I have a few questions for you, Mr. Grayson."

Though Grayson continued to maintain his welcoming smile, there was a complacency to it that existed just along the perimeter. He thought himself superior, Hawk realized. That was fine with him. As long as the man thought he had the upper hand, he wouldn't be that aware that he was being taken down.

"Everyone does," he told Hawk easily. "I'll do my best to answer them for you. In just one moment," he said, holding up his finger to indicated that he wanted his "guest" to pause his thoughts. "Carly, I'm going to need to see your lesson plan for tomorrow's children seminar," he told her. "If you don't mind, I'd like you to drop it off in my office later this evening. Say around nine?" he suggested, eyeing her. Waiting for her compliance.

"Of course, Samuel. Nine will be fine," she replied in the same obedient, subservient tone that her sister had.

Turning back to Hawk, Grayson clasped his hands together before him and said, "Now then, you said you have some questions for me?"

He had questions all right. Foremost was why did Grayson want to see Carly in his office later this evening? Was he just asking her to drop off the papers, or did he have something else in mind for her?

Though he gave no outward indication, Hawk could

feel anger flare within him. It took a great deal to keep it under control.

Forcing himself to focus on the present, Hawk opened up the manila envelope he had brought with him. As Grayson watched with what he took to be feigned interest, he removed five eight-by-ten photographs, one for each of the women who had been found.

"We're investigating the deaths of these five women," he told Grayson, deliberately substituting the word *deaths* for *murders.* One by one, he shuffled through them, displaying each for Grayson's benefit. He watched the man's face intently. "Do you recognize any of them?" he asked.

Grayson dutifully viewed one photograph after another. His expression never changed, and he gave no indication that he recognized any of the women.

Even so, Hawk could have sworn that the small, blue vein at the man's right temple pulsed as he looked down at the photographs. There was genuine surprise registered there, he thought. Apparently Grayson hadn't thought that these bodies would ever surface.

But he knew them. Hawk would bet his soul on that. Grayson knew each of these women, including their mysterious Jane Doe. Getting him to admit it, though, would be difficult if not impossible.

He needed someone on the inside to bear witness against the man.

Shaking his head, Grayson returned the photographs. "I'm afraid I really can't be of any help to you. I don't recall meeting any of these unfortunate ladies. The faces from my past tend to run together."

I just bet they do, Hawk thought, taking the photographs back and slipping them into the envelope again.

"I have seen so many people—I started out as a motivational speaker, you know," Grayson explained in an aside. "That was before I found my true calling." His hands swept about, indicating the now-empty auditorium.

Hawk continued to watch the man's face, looking for a breech, some telltale sign, however small, to give him a clue to his real intent in taking over Cold Plains. "And that would be?"

"Why, leaving my mark on this wonderful town, of course. Making sure that it is developed to meet its full potential, so that everyone here might benefit. You're free to move about, you know, Special Agent, so you can see for yourself how business is thriving and how well and happy everyone who lives here is. I'd like to think I had some small part in that," he added with studied modesty.

Had the so-called spiritual leader just inadvertently admitted to eliminating the people who weren't "well and happy?" Hawk wondered, because they clearly weren't out and about. Everyone he'd seen so far had the same frozen, unnerving smile plastered on their faces as if anything else was strictly forbidden.

Hawk took the opening to ask, "I've noticed that nobody here seems to be sick. No colds, no allergies…" He allowed his voice to trail off, curious as to what the other man would say.

Grayson laughed. "Well, we've decided to outlaw all that."

He made it sound like a joke, but Hawk had an uneasy feeling that the man wasn't really kidding. It was all about *his* choices, *his* preferences, *his* master plan. Whether he made light of it or not, Grayson was convinced that the world revolved around him—as it should.

Hell, it was clear that Grayson really did think he was God.

Chapter 11

She wasn't home.

There were no lights on in the eighty-year-old farmhouse, and her car was nowhere to be seen. He'd knocked three times, anyway, each time a little louder than the last. Each time with the same results.

There was no answer.

Hawk remained at her front door another minute or so. Then frustrated, he turned on his heel and walked away.

But rather than just shrug it off and proceed on to his hotel room for the night, Hawk got into his car and sat there in the dark, waiting. As he waited, he grew progressively restless and apprehensive with each minute that ticked by.

Where the hell was she?

Carly had told him that she didn't stay in town, that

she liked sleeping here, in her own bed, where she felt she had some sort of control over her immediate surroundings. In Cold Plains, the ever-increasing number of Devotees of Samuel, as the "faithful" sometimes referred to themselves, made her feel uncomfortable, so she preferred to do her sleeping here. He could well understand that.

Hawk tried to distract himself by reviewing the information he had on hand, but his mind kept going back to the fact that he'd heard Samuel asking Carly to come by his office once he finished in the auditorium.

Again, Hawk uneasily wondered why. A series of scenarios kept suggesting themselves in his head, but he blocked them before any of them could completely materialize.

Maybe he should have hung around himself, Hawk thought. His presence, he was certain, would have been taken as a silent warning to Grayson that he wasn't to harm anyone or have any of his henchmen harm anyone. Because if he did, everything the self-enamored egotist had built up would come crashing down around his ears faster than a child's plastic building blocks.

With a frustrated sigh, Hawk debated starting his car and going back to town.

But if he left now, he might wind up missing Carly if she came to the farmhouse via another route. And if he burst in on Grayson in his office or where he lived, that would completely blow the mission. He didn't want Grayson alerted to the fact that he and his people were under FBI surveillance. So far, all the so-called charismatic leader thought was that he was some independent FBI agent asking questions about a bunch of dead women and not getting any useful answers in reply.

The longer he sat in the dark with his imagination attempting to run amuck, the less reasonable and patient Hawk became. He thought about calling Jeffers or Patterson and sending the agent into town to look around, but that, too, would arouse suspicions. Cold Plains wasn't exactly the kind of town that received a steady flow of outside traffic. It was neither a tourist draw—although from what he'd picked up that was apparently part of Grayson's plan—nor on the road to somewhere else. There would be no reason for a stranger to pass through without a specific reason.

Hell, he didn't care if it made sense or not. She could be in some kind of real danger while he sat here, as inert as Hamlet mumbling his "to be or not to be" soliloquy to himself.

Fed up with waiting, Hawk was just about to start his vehicle when he saw headlights slicing through the darkened terrain. Removing his key from the ignition, he watched as they drew closer and the car became larger.

It was Carly's car. He recognized her headlights. The right one was slightly dimmer than the left. While he wanted to leap out of his own vehicle to ask her why she was so late, he forced himself to remain where he was and calm down.

Number one, he had no right to make noises like some overwrought, jealous boyfriend, and number two, the fact that she might not be alone—something that truly bothered him—would make his sudden appear-

ance difficult to explain to whomever was with her—
especially if it turned out to be either Grayson or one
of his many minions.

So Hawk stayed where he was and impatiently
waited. And watched.

When Carly pulled her car up in front of the farmhouse and got out, she was alone.

The second he was sure of that, Hawk shot out of his
own vehicle like a hastily fired bullet and cut across
the front yard. Taking the porch steps two at a time, he
caught up to Carly just as she reached the front door.

Startled, she swung around, her fist drawn back like
a prize-fighter in training. She stopped two inches short
of making contact and dropped her hand when she saw
who it was.

"What are you doing here?" she asked. Damn but this
man was going to wind up giving her a heart attack yet.

"Checking on you," Hawk replied, his tone decep-
tively simple.

She'd been too preoccupied as she approached the
house and hadn't noticed his car parked outside. Carly
drew in a deep breath, then let it go, doing her best to
calm her rather shaky nerves. It didn't really work. She
tried again.

Unlocking the door, she let Hawk inside. "Why?" she
asked wearily. "Are you afraid that I'll suddenly turn
into a Samuel groupie?"

Alerted by her tone that something was off, Hawk
moved around to get in front of her. He wanted a better
look at her face as she turned on the light. Taking her
chin in his hand, he examined her even more closely.

Carly tried to turn her head away, but he held her captive.

"You know better than that," he told her. His eyes slid over her face. Something was wrong. "What happened tonight?"

Carly let out a huge, soul-twisting sigh before answering.

"Nothing." Then raising her eyes to his, she added, "At least not the way you mean, anyway."

Hawk couldn't decide if she was telling him the truth, or merely trying to spare him because that was the kind of person she was, ready to shoulder rather than share the burden. Even when its weight could very possibly break her.

"Grayson didn't touch you?" Hawk demanded.

The small, disparaging laugh had no humor to it. "Oh, he touched me, all right." The next moment, Hawk looked as if he would go charging out the door. She grabbed his arm to stop him from letting his emotions get the better of his common sense. "But again, not the way you mean."

His temper frayed into combustible strips, Hawk shouted, "Then for heaven's sakes, tell me what *you* mean." The next moment, his better judgment resurfaced and he realized that he owed her an apology for acting like a Neanderthal. "Sorry. I didn't mean to start shouting at you."

She knew he wasn't shouting at her, but shouting at Grayson by proxy. The frustration that his hands were temporarily tied had gotten the better of him.

"Apology accepted," she said, leading the way to

the kitchen. "Why don't you sit down?" she suggested, nodding at the table. "I'll make us some tea and tell you what happened."

She was the one who looked as if she needed to be waited on, he judged. "No, you sit down, and I'll make the tea," Hawk offered, reversing the order. "But you *can* tell me what happened."

"Done," she answered with a faint smile. She all but bonelessly slid onto the kitchen chair. For one second, Carly fought the urge to put her head down on the table and just make this evening, as well as the world in general, go away for a little while. She'd been caught unaware, but she'd gotten through it, and that was all that mattered.

Hawk was waiting for her. Taking another breath, she began her narrative of the evening's events, trying to be as succinct as possible. "Grayson decided to welcome me into the fold."

Hawk took the battered, red tea kettle from the back of the stove and brought it over to the sink. Turning on the faucet, he started to fill the kettle with water.

"What does that mean?" he asked guardedly, doing his best to sound calm. The trouble was, where Carly was involved, he had a tendency to remain anything *but* calm.

"He made a devotee out of me," Carly replied quietly, turning her face away from him. She stared out the kitchen window, into the darkness just beyond.

"He indoctrinated you?" Hawk asked uneasily as he put the kettle on the front burner and switched on the gas jet beneath it. Small, blue flames popped up and danced feverishly beneath the round metal surface.

"He tattooed me," she replied through teeth that were slightly shy of being clenched.

The kettle and its contents were forgotten. Hawk came around to where she was sitting and dropped to his knees before her. He knew what she was saying, but he was hoping that, by some fluke, he was wrong.

"You mean…?"

Carly silently nodded. It was stupid to cry, and she didn't want to. She wanted to yell, to be angry—and she was—but tears came to her eyes, anyway. Upbraiding herself for this weak display didn't stem their flow.

She pressed her lips together, drew back the wide, billowing beige skirt from her leg and pulled the material up high so that her right thigh was completely exposed for Hawk to see.

On it was a small, fresh, black letter *D*. The skin just beneath it was an angry red. Hawk cringed when he saw it. He swore he could feel the same needle inking his flesh.

As if his brain was on a five-second delay, he suddenly heard what she'd said. "He does the tattoo himself?" Hawk asked, surprised.

Carly nodded, telling herself that once this was over and behind her, she would have the tattoo removed, no matter what it took or how painful that process turned out to be.

"Seems to really enjoy doing it, too," she told him grimly. "Enjoys the fact that he was inflicting pain 'artistically.'"

Hawk rocked back on his heels, suddenly struck by a thought. What she'd just told him was a brand-new piece of information they hadn't had before. A few tiny pieces of the puzzle came together.

"That's probably why," he said.

Carly looked at him, confused. Was he talking to himself or to her? "What's probably why?"

He glanced up. It made sense now. "I think I know why our Jane Doe was killed. She had a black *D* on her hip, except that hers was done with a black marker. She undoubtedly did it in order to blend in. But she didn't know that the only one who 'awarded' those tattoos was Grayson himself."

As the light dawned, Carly finished his statement for him. "So when he saw it, Grayson knew she had to be an imposter."

"Right, which naturally made him suspicious. Because of what he felt was at stake, he didn't stop to ask her any questions, he just had her executed." That still didn't tell him what the woman was doing there in the first place, but at least they had one of the answers.

"Executed?" Carly echoed uncertainly, clearly confused.

Hawk nodded. "That was a detail we kept back from the media." That way, if a copycat killer suddenly emerged, they would be aware of it. He had no doubts a great many sick people existed who would do anything for their fifteen minutes of fame—or infamy in this case. "Each of the women was shot in the back of the head. A single bullet, execution style."

It didn't necessarily have to be an execution, she

thought. "Or shot when they weren't looking, so they didn't know what was coming—or get the chance to plead for their lives," she suggested.

He hadn't thought of that. Hawk looked at Carly with a flicker of admiration. "That's a possibility, too," he agreed, then grinned. "Not bad."

"Thank you." He saw a small smile struggling to emerge.

The tea kettle began to whistle, calling attention to itself and the water that was now boiling madly. Hawk rose to his feet again and crossed back to the stove. He opened a couple of cupboards before he finally located two large mugs.

"He asked me, you know," she told him, watching Hawk as he poured steaming hot water into the mugs. "Grayson asked if I was serious about becoming one of his 'chosen followers.' If I'd said no or that I had to think about it, he would have slammed the proverbial door in my face, just like that—" she snapped her fingers "—and then I probably wouldn't even be able to get in contact with Mia or talk to her."

Carly sounded almost a little defensive. After what she'd just been through, did she think he was going to give her a hard time? He wasn't completely heartless.

"You don't have to explain anything to me, Carly," he told her.

She would beg to differ, Carly thought. "The expression on your face when you came up behind me just now said that I do. You looked damn angry that I was late getting home."

He shrugged, his shoulder vaguely moving up and down. "I was worried about you."

Carly relaxed a little. *I was worried about you.* That had a nice ring to it.

Carly knew that it didn't really mean anything in the grand scheme of things, because life had taken them in different directions—*since you sent him away,* her mind taunted—and even though their paths had crossed one another temporarily, life would soon be back on its rightful track, and he would have his life and she hers.

But his voiced concern still sounded nice, and just for the slightest moment, Carly indulged herself by letting her mind go to the land of what-if?

What if she hadn't sent him away? What if he'd stayed by choice? Or she had been able to leave without her conscience bleeding, anchoring her here?

What if…?

Snapping out of it, Carly said, "It's been a long while since anyone was worried about me."

He knew how independent she'd always been and, thank God, apparently still was, despite her pretense to the contrary for Grayson's benefit. Truth of it was, he wasn't all that certain what he would have ultimately done if she really had turned out to be one of Grayson's followers.

Probably tried to kidnap her the way she was trying to find a way of kidnapping Mia as a last resort, he thought.

Out loud he said, "Sorry, didn't mean to crowd you or infer that you weren't perfectly capable of taking care of yourself." The words were automatic rather than straight from the heart—the way his flash of anger had been. "No offense intended."

He was backing away. Why? Did he think she wanted him to? Or was it that he didn't want her thinking that there was something still between them when there clearly wasn't?

"None taken," she murmured.

Coming to, he picked up both steaming mugs and crossed back to the table. He placed one in front of her, then placed the second one on the table where he was sitting. He slipped back onto his chair.

Carly looked down at Hawk's masterpiece and then grinned. The man had forgotten one key ingredient.

"You know," she began gently, "it might help to put the tea bags in."

His attention had been completely focused on her, and he'd been grappling with surges of anger and the very strong desire to strangle the man he had under surveillance. Case or no case, when he thought of the man possibly forcing himself on Carly, all bets were off. In that tiny space of time, he was a man first and an FBI special agent second.

Not something his superiors would be thrilled about hearing.

He glanced down at the two mugs. Each was filled to the brim with water. Tea bags, however, were nowhere in sight. He'd forgotten to put them in. He would obviously never make it as a waiter, he thought ruefully.

"Sorry," Hawk muttered under his breath as he started to get up again.

Carly stopped him by putting her hand on top of his.

When he eyed her quizzically, she nodded at his chair and indicated that he should sit down again.

"You sit, I'll get the tea bags," she told him. "I know where they are," she added. "You'll only wind up having to go searching through the pantry," she told him with a soft laugh.

They were right where she'd left them. But when Carly turned away from the pantry, the tin with tea bags in her hand, she found that Hawk wasn't where she had left *him.*

He was right behind her, so close that when she'd turned around, her body had brushed against his. She felt the electric tingle immediately. It blotted out the revulsion she'd been battling with.

"Are you that impatient for tea?" she asked, trying to suppress a grin.

Her eyes were dancing, he noted. And all he wanted to do right at this moment was make her his again.

"The hell with the tea," he answered. His emotions were still all in a jumble, and he was at a loss how to sort everything all out. "I thought that Grayson—I was afraid that you—"

None of this was coming out right. He wasn't accustomed to feeling this confused, as if he was being pulled in two directions at the same time, one labeled duty, the other labeled conscience. And him stuck in the middle.

"Damn it, Carly," he all but exploded, thinking of what *might* have happened to her had Grayson an inkling that she was playing him, "I don't like you taking these kinds of chances."

She knew that, but she still found it oddly comforting to hear him admit it.

"You don't have the right to tell me not to do this, you know," she reminded him, even though she couldn't suppress the hint of a smile curving her lips.

"I know," he answered, "but just thinking that something could have happened to you—"

Hawk couldn't bring himself to finish his sentence. Instead, he abruptly pulled her into his arms and kissed her. Kissed her hard, with all the feeling pulsing through his body.

It took Carly a full thirty seconds to find her breath. "The water's going to get cold," she whispered, not trusting her voice to keep from cracking if she spoke any louder.

He didn't care about the damn tea. "It can be reheated."

His words brought a wide smile to her lips. "Apparently," Carly said with a soft laugh as she pressed her body against his, "so can you."

He brought his mouth down on hers again, this time with even more force than before. Kissing her as if there was no tomorrow because, for all he knew, there wasn't one.

Not for him, not for her and especially not for them.

Chapter 12

Hawk had long ago decided that law enforcement work was a combination of danger and boredom with very little in between. On rare occasions, there was also a glimmer of the satisfaction associated with closing a case. But for the most part, it was the former set of circumstances that prevailed.

The boredom also included more than a little frustration. There was no doubt in Hawk's mind that this particular case, involving dead women and a rampant display of mind control, was the classic example of both of those elements.

It was clearly dangerous because if Samuel Grayson decided that he had become a threat to his utopia, Grayson would have him eliminated without a thought. The frustration in this case was multifaceted, like a Hydra monster straight out of Greek mythology. Hawk found himself frustrated at almost every turn he took. There was the matter of the second victim's, currently Jane Doe's, true identity. She matched no missing persons report or any of the fingerprints that were on file in the various databases.

And as of this moment, the facial recognition program, which Jeffers had been running non-stop for the past day and a half, hadn't found a match, either.

If this woman *was* an undercover operative, it had to be deep cover because, to date, no agency had attempted to claim her.

Maybe the woman had been a private detective, hired to track down and bring back someone Grayson had attracted to his community and subsequently brainwashed. It was a possibility. Hawk had suggested it to Jeffers the instant he thought of it.

"If she was a private investigator," Jeffers had pointed out, "then she'd have to have a license and her prints would be on file somewhere—which they're not," he concluded with a deep sigh.

The only other possibility, Hawk had gone on to speculate, was that the woman *hadn't* been a professional investigator and had undertaken this "going undercover" mission on her own because someone she cared about had been absorbed into Grayson's society.

Their Jane Doe could have very well acted on the same instincts that Carly had, Hawk realized the next moment. The thought was far from comforting.

Damn but he wished he could get Carly to listen to him and give up this charade. He didn't want her turning up in some shallow grave just because her sister was one of the mindless and addle brained who was so hopelessly devoted to Grayson.

Driving through the town like a man strictly out to enjoy the afternoon, Hawk observed the town's citizens, looking for evidence he could work with.

He wasn't sure just how much longer he could keep his mouth shut around Carly about the role she was playing. He made a right at the next corner with the intentions of doing one last round. He'd made his initial protest to her, then had intended to let the matter go because Carly wouldn't be browbeaten or bullied into backing away. When pushed, she had a tendency to dig in, not flee or relent. He'd learned that a long time ago when her father had taunted her that she would never amount to anything. She became the only reason they didn't lose the farm years ago.

But knowing the way she reacted didn't keep him from voicing his opinion rather loudly the other night when he'd thought something had happened to her.

In a way, it had, he reminded himself. She'd been tattooed—branded—by that sick S.O.B. Hawk was now more worried than ever about her safety. Grayson was paying too much attention to her. Whether it was because he was suspicious that she wasn't on the level or because he had singled her out as one of his particular "favorites," Hawk didn't know, and it really made no difference to him. The end result was the same. It placed Carly in danger.

And he didn't like it.

One way or the other, he *had* to get her to leave town for her own good. Even if, by getting her to leave, he would be getting rid of the one bright spot in his life—not just here but in general.

For the past ten years, Hawk had been all about the job, all about his duty and whatever case he was working on. Nothing distracted him, nothing divided his focus. He'd had no real personal life, moreover, no desire to open up that part of himself where his feelings had once resided.

But being with Carly this short space of time, whether he liked it or not, had abruptly changed all that. It made him remember that there was another side to life, a side that didn't involve guns, dead bodies and covert operations.

A side that involved a reason to smile.

Don't get used to this, Hawk silently ordered himself. All of this—the good part—would be in his past in what amounted to less than the blink of an eye. And the less he invested himself in it now, the easier it would be for him to regroup and move on later. He needed to remember that.

"Words to live by," he said sarcastically, under his breath.

The other source of his frustration, currently at the top of his list, was trying to reach Micah. For three weeks now he'd had the same kind of luck: none.

It was as if the man had just disappeared off the face of the earth after that initial communication.

Or, Hawk thought grimly, Micah's brother had had him killed, just like, he was certain, Grayson'd had everyone else who had incurred his displeasure killed.

If that did turn out to be the case, he had no idea

where to begin looking for Micah Grayson's body—other than perhaps in or around the town where Micah had arranged to meet him, he supposed. Still, that was a large area to cover.

Could Grayson have learned about the proposed meeting, seen it as a threat to what he was doing and sent one of his henchmen to eliminate his twin brother? He might have even done it himself, Hawk speculated. Grayson might have taken a certain pleasure in ridding the world of his double, so that there was and would continue to be only *one* person with his face.

Who knew what went through that psychopath's mind, Hawk thought, his frustration mounting as he felt that he was facing yet another brick wall.

There just had to be some faster way to get answers, but for the life of him, Hawk didn't know how.

Carly struggled to keep her smile pasted to her lips. It was far from easy. Not when she was standing in the doorway of the community center's all-purpose room, looking at the ongoing preparations for Mia's upcoming wedding.

Samuel had put several of his more dedicated female followers to work, festively decorating the area. They went about their appointed tasks, fashioning roses out of construction paper and adding gaily-colored streamers to every square inch of the community room.

To Carly, it looked as if a colored paper mill had exploded. In addition to streamers, balloons would soon flood the room. Because of helium's somewhat limited life span, the balloons would be brought in during the last leg of the preparations so that they would appear robust and full of promise on the big day.

Unlike the actual situation.

When one of the women looked up and saw her, Carly suddenly found herself being pressed into service, despite her protests. After all, she was the sister of the bride. Her sense of pride and loyalty should have had her insisting on helping right from the beginning, one of the volunteers, a woman named Janice told her in no uncertain terms.

Carly would have liked nothing more than to leave—for a number of reasons, most prominently her incredibly strong disapproval of this match. But she knew it would look suspicious if she flatly declined Bubblehead Lady's tersely worded suggestion. And that in turn would only wind up calling for a closer scrutiny of her behavior.

So she forced herself to cheerfully say, "Of course," in response to Janice's urgings to "Come help us get ready for Mia's wedding."

She'd give them an hour, Carly decided, then beg off to run some imaginary errand. They couldn't find fault with that, right?

Mentally she began the countdown.

And in the meantime, she worked to create paper wild roses—pink ones—and she listened. She didn't have to listen for very long to hear something distasteful.

"Mia is so lucky that Brice Carrington chose her—and that Samuel approved," one of the other women declared.

And still another agreed, saying, "Brice is quite a catch, you know." She turned her brown eyes to look at Carly. "Any one of the unattached ladies would have been more than thrilled if they had caught his eye. But Samuel thinks that your sister is best suited for him. Samuel says that she is at a perfect age as well as being physically perfect," the woman confided, leaning in toward Carly to "share" her information.

A third woman chimed in, "Samuel believes your sister will make beautiful, healthy devotees."

"Perhaps six, if not more," Janice spouted as if she was repeating the gospel of her lord. Her eyes swept over the others and, for a moment, lingered on Carly as if she was waiting to be contradicted or challenged.

A baby machine, Carly thought with contempt. *Grayson doesn't see Mia as a person, he sees her as some kind of a soulless baby machine for him to operate. I was right all along,* she thought angrily, finding no solace in having guessed correctly.

With all her heart, she wished that Mia could hear this. Maybe *then* she would finally snap out of her trance, see things for what they really were. But this seemed a hopeless venture. Her sister clearly bought into Grayson's vision of the world and was perfectly comfortable with the man's plans for her future.

That only left kidnapping her sister as an option.

Since Mia remained in town each night, she would have to keep her eyes open for an available opportunity to abduct Mia without being noticed or arousing suspicion.

She hated thinking about it, but there was obviously no other way.

In addition to finding the right opportunity to get this all to snap into gear, Carly would probably have to bound and gag Mia in order to get her out of here. Otherwise, her sister was liable to scream her head off and get them both killed.

Or at least her, Carly thought cynically.

Sometime during working on this forced "labor of love," it occurred to Carly that one of the faces she'd become accustomed to seeing around town, and especially around the community center, was missing today.

Now that she thought about it, she hadn't seen the young woman in at least a couple of days. Maybe even longer. With her relationship with Hawk heating up so unexpectedly and so quickly, she'd wound up overlooking everything that wasn't directly connected to Mia.

"Where's Susannah?" she asked the women now, hoping one of them could fill her in. What she hadn't expected was sarcasm.

"Ah, she speaks. I thought maybe you'd gone mute," Janice told her coolly as she worked.

Carly deliberately kept her tone amiable. "I didn't want to interrupt any of you ladies while you were talking," Carly replied, hiding her resentment at the comment.

Besides, she'd found that listening to the people around her talk—if they were Grayson's followers—was far more informative than talking herself.

The woman she was asking about wasn't like any of these women she was working with. Or for that matter, she wasn't like most of the women in town. Susannah Paul was a sweet, young woman with a rather lost, haunted look in her eyes. It was that look that had first drawn her to Susannah. Once they spoke, there was almost an instant bond. Carly had found herself befriending the brand-new mother who had confided to her just the other day that she was having second thoughts about living here under what felt like "Samuel's watchful eye." She'd whispered that it made her feel uneasy.

Carly had tried to be sympathetic without tipping her own hand. She remembered urging Susannah not to do anything hasty without letting her know first.

"I don't want you feeling alone," she had explained. "Or going off by yourself with your baby." Squeezing the young woman's hand, she'd said with all sincerity, "I want to help you if I can. I know it can't be easy, being a single mother with a brand-new baby."

She'd seen a little of herself in that scenario, because after their mother had died, she had all but raised Mia on her own, too. Certainly her drunken father hadn't been of any actual help when it came to that. The only thing the man knew how to do was how to drink, not how to raise a very young girl.

In response to her words, Susannah had given her a quick, grateful smile and had promised to keep her apprised of any decisions she would make.

"You'll be the first one I'll tell," she'd said. "And probably the only one, too."

So where was she?

Carly looked at Janice, waiting for the woman's

answer since she seemed to be into everyone's business. But instead of responding, the woman looked up uneasily, making eye contact with someone behind her.

The next moment, Carly heard Samuel's deep voice saying, "Please don't trouble yourself about Susannah." She turned around to face the man just as he said, "She is where she is supposed to be."

That didn't sound good, Carly couldn't help thinking. "And that is—?" she pressed.

Grayson gave her a beatific smile. "—none of your concern," the man concluded serenely.

Suppressing a sense of horror, Carly still couldn't make herself let it go. "And the baby?" she whispered, almost afraid of the answer.

"Why, with her, of course," Samuel replied. "Where else would a young child be, but with the woman who had given her life?"

Carly's blood ran cold, all but draining from her face. Could Grayson possibly be saying that Susannah and her precious baby were dead? That maybe he had learned that she was vacillating about continuing under his so-called guidance.

Considering his low opinion of people, Susannah's doubts about remaining in Cold Plains and involved in the center made her imperfect in Grayson's eyes, and Carly was beginning to see what the man did with anyone who he deemed imperfect.

Samuel's eyes narrowed, and he made no attempt to hide the fact that he was scrutinizing her as if trying to delve into her thoughts. "Why are you so interested in where Susannah is, Carly?"

"I just thought I could help her take care of the baby," Carly explained innocently. "She seemed a little overwhelmed."

"My perception of her exactly," Samuel agreed with a vigorous nod of his head. The smile he gave her made Carly feel *really* uneasy. "We seem to think alike, Carly, you and I." His eyes were all but holding her prisoner. "I find that very gratifying."

Carly knew enough to pretend to look down demurely. It was either that or have him see how much she truly hated him for having brought so much evil to her home.

He looked as if he was about to suggest that they continue their "talk" and comparison of thoughts in his office.

She was saved at the last minute. Because just then, someone called to Grayson about needing his final input on several pressing matters involving the construction of yet another new building along Cold Plains's Main street.

"Duty calls," Grayson told her with a heavy, dramatic sigh as he excused himself from her company. Then just before he left, he leaned over and whispered in her ear. "This conversation is far from over, Carly," he promised.

As he left the room, the women all looked at her with unabashed envy.

Feeling as if she had just dodged a bullet, Carly made herself scarce as quickly as possible. She needed to get away from town, away from Grayson, at least until she figured out how to handle all this unwanted attention.

The man clearly wanted to brand her with more than just the letter *D* that he had tattooed onto her thigh.

"She's missing," Carly announced to Hawk when she let him into her house later that evening.

She had given him a spare key, but Hawk thought it more prudent if he knocked and waited for her to open the door. That way, she would see that it was him, and she couldn't be caught by surprise by anyone else if they attempted to break in on her.

"Mia?" he guessed, since she hadn't mentioned the missing woman's name.

"No, Susannah Paul." Carly could see that the name meant nothing to him. Why should it? As far as she knew, Susannah hadn't spoke to him. Susannah knew nothing about nothing, so there would have been no reason for her to speak with the FBI special agent. "She told me she was thinking about leaving the community."

Well, maybe that was her answer, Hawk thought, following her to the kitchen. Every night since he'd made that first stop to "check" on her, he'd stop to have a little dinner with her and then stay to talk. Except that they hardly ever did. They let their passion do the talking for them.

"Maybe she did," he speculated, but he could see why she was concerned. People didn't just up and leave Cold Plains, not unless Grayson wanted them to. And then it was as if the atmosphere had just swallowed them up.

Carly shook her head. "Susannah wouldn't go without telling me. I made her promise she'd let me know first. And there's something else."

Hawk looked at her, waiting.

"She's just had a baby recently. She wouldn't really be up for a lot of traveling." She glanced at Hawk, but long enough so that he could see the distress in her eyes. God knew, it wasn't without merit.

Carly hesitated for a moment, then asked, "Do you think that Grayson could have—"

"He very well could have, yes, but don't let your imagination go there yet. There could still be a lot of other plausible explanations," he told her soothingly.

But even as he said it, he wasn't nearly as convinced as he sounded for Carly's benefit.

And he suspected that Carly knew it, too.

Chapter 13

Carly was running out of time and she knew it.

Mia's wedding ceremony was less than three days away. For the past two days, she hadn't even been able to get *near* her sister.

Each time she tried, Mia was either already busy working under Grayson's watchful guidance, or if her sister appeared to be momentarily alone and she started to approach her, Grayson would somehow suddenly come swooping down out of nowhere, requesting that Mia join him or come see something, or he'd use a dozen and one other diversion tactics to separate Mia from everyone else.

Mainly her.

Not that she had much hope of miraculously persuading her sister to give up this absurd idea of marrying a man who was more than twice her age. The last time she had gotten to talk to her alone, she had used every argument she could think of to persuade Mia not to make what she considered in her heart to be a "terrible mistake."

Mia hadn't even let her finish. Her sister had looked at her with open hostility and said, "I don't care if you like what Cold Plains has become or not, but I do. I *like* it here, do you understand? For the first time in my life, I have order, I have peace—and I have a place that makes me feel as if I'm important." She'd raised her chin pugnaciously and declared, "For the first time in my life, I feel happy."

For the first time in my life.

That had stung. Badly.

Carly tried hard not to make it about hurt feelings, but it was difficult not to. She had sacrificed everything for her sister, especially her own happiness. She had stayed on here in Cold Plains when she would have much rather just taken off and started a brand-new life with Hawk.

"And you didn't before?" she had challenged Mia with suppressed anger.

Mia had tossed her head, her eyes narrowing as she had looked at her defiantly. "No."

"And life with me was so terrible?" Carly asked.

"What 'with' you?" Mia demanded, throwing up her hands. She upset one of the decorations that had just been hung up that morning. Angry, she picked it up and lovingly dusted it off before carefully reattaching it. "I never saw you," she pointed out accusingly.

How could Mia stand there, throwing that into her

face? There was a reason she hadn't been around and it wasn't because she was out having a good time, enjoying herself. She had run herself ragged, trying to make ends meet.

Didn't her sister understand that?

Apparently not, she concluded. Sighing, Carly gave it her all, trying one more time to reason with Mia.

"That's because I was trying to run the farm and earn some money on the side as a waitress so you could have the little luxuries, you know, like food." She realized that came out sounding rather sarcastic. She hadn't meant for it to, but she was still stunned that, given all those years she'd worked so hard so that her sister could have at least a few things that she hadn't had, Mia wasn't grateful for any of it.

"I would have rather had you," Mia spat out. "I never got to talk to anyone. You were *never* there for me." Her eyes became angry blue flames. "All I ever did was clean up after Dad. And I mean that literally."

"So did I," Carly informed her. They stood facing one another, officially at a standoff. "I worked so that you could have regular meals, clothes on your back, a roof over your head. If I hadn't done what I did, we would have lost the family farm."

Mia drew herself up and went back to working on the decorations for her wedding. "So now I hope you and the farm will be very happy together. And if you can't be happy for me at my wedding," she added curtly, "then don't bother coming. The choice is yours."

Carly stared at the back of her sister's head. How could Mia talk to her this way? How could she be so insensitive as not to see everything she'd given up for her?

"Mia, I—"

"There you are!" a cheerful voice addressing Mia declared.

Charlie Rhodes, one of Grayson's inner circle of handpicked men, who was also going to be best man at the wedding, came up behind them and then took Mia gently by the arm.

At first glance, Charlie had the features of a sweet-faced angel.

He probably would have been one of the fallen ones, Carly couldn't help thinking. In the few, brief exchanges they'd had, Charlie had been nothing but polite to her, but she still couldn't get over the uneasy feeling she would always get in the pit of her stomach whenever she was around the young man. For one thing, his eyes were flat, as if there was no soul, no conscience, behind them.

"Samuel's been looking for you," Charlie told Mia. "He has something to ask you about those children's seminars you've been giving for him. He seemed pretty busy, so I offered to fetch you for him."

Fetch. Just like she was some inanimate object, Carly thought. *Mia, wise up! Please!*

"Well, you found me," Mia declared cheerfully. "Now take me to him."

Said the lamb to the wolf as she was led off to the slaughter. Damn it, Mia, don't you hear *yourself?* Carly wondered angrily.

For a moment, she thought about just grabbing Mia's

hand and running, but she knew how irrational that would seem. For one thing, Mia wouldn't run with her, certainly not willingly. She'd probably just dig in her heels and refuse to go.

That had been her last one-on-one contact with her sister, almost five days ago. Since then, every attempt she'd made had been thwarted one way or another. She may actually have to kidnap Mia and get her out of the community. There appeared to be no other way to save her.

That evening when she came home, she was still contemplating the exact logistics of pulling off her sister's kidnapping. Everything she came up with depended heavily on luck. The only easy part was getting into the compound, and that was because Samuel believed her to be just as brainwashed as the others.

When she'd resisted moving into town, he'd been a little suspicious at first, his hypnotic eyes all but burrowing into her. But she had pointed out that she needed to keep the farm in business. After all, her chickens did provide breakfast for the masses and her dairy cows kept the children in milk.

Using that as her foundation, Carly managed to convince Samuel that she could better serve the community by returning to the farm each evening and working it the hours she was not teaching the children.

So with Grayson thinking she was one of the true believers, she had the element of surprise on her side. That would win her about sixty seconds. After that, she would have to run like crazy, dragging her sister behind her. Either that or get to her just before the ceremony. Ultimately, the plans were the same. One way or another, she intended to abduct Mia before her little sister had a chance to say those fatal words that would seal her doom.

Carly pulled her car up near the house and looked around. Disappointment nudged its way to the surface and hung there. She worked her lower lip uneasily. There was no trace of Hawk.

Funny how quickly that man got to be a habit with her. All it took was looking at him, and she was a goner. He'd been her first love and, as it had turned out, her only love. She had never felt anything for any other man. Not that she had actively tried to find someone, but once or twice, she'd gone out with one of the other men in town. Her ultimate goal had been to find some sort of companionship. Maybe even settle down.

But for her, there was no repeat performance of a magic moment, no chemistry suddenly pulsating through her. Not even the desire to be held and kissed by whoever was taking her out that night.

And so she eventually came to the inevitable conclusion that Hawk would forever be the one and only man she would ever care about, ever love.

And he was out of her life by her own doing.

She had to resign herself to that. So she did.

Until he'd shown up, Carly thought now, letting herself into the darkened house. He had instantly turned her whole world upside down by coming back into town, looking better than any man had a right to after ten years had gone by.

This time, she didn't know how she would survive having him walk away. Because he would. He'd carved out that life for himself that she'd pushed him toward.

A life that didn't include her.

"Don't think that far ahead," she chided herself. "He's still here for now, and all any of us have is now. Make the most of it," she ordered herself as she went around the house, turning on lights and chasing away the gloom.

With the house now well lit, Carly made her way into the kitchen to prepare dinner. It seemed rather ironic because she hardly bothered with dinner when she was alone. Usually it meant just grabbing something out of the refrigerator and eating it over the sink while doing three other things at the same time.

But for Hawk, she prepared dinner. Looked forward to dinner. Even if they didn't speak, she still loved to sit there beside him at the table, watching him eat what she'd made for him. Doing so gave her a warm feeling of normalcy she'd been lacking for longer than she could actually remember.

Maybe that was why Mia wanted to get married, Carly thought abruptly. Why her sister seemed to cleave to this sham of a life she saw being offered to her. Because she wanted what everyone wanted. A little piece of the normal life.

Except that marriage to Brice Carrington wouldn't be normal. Not in the way Mia wanted in her heart. Mia would be nothing more than a baby machine.

After taking the roast she'd made yesterday out of the refrigerator, Carly glanced at her watch. What was keeping Hawk? Not that there was a specific time that had been agreed upon. It was just that Hawk was usually here by now.

Leaving the roast on the counter, Carly suddenly felt an uneasy need to watch for him through the large bay window that faced her private road. The road that led away from the heart of Cold Plains.

Carly picked up her pace and made her way to the living room.

She passed by the gun rack where she still kept her late father's weapons primed and cleaned. They represented the only really good memory she had of the man. On the occasions that he'd been sober when she was a child, her father had tried to take her hunting. When she'd burst into tears the first time because he'd told her they were going to hunt for deer, he'd relented and taught her how to shoot at targets instead. She wound up shooting at pictures of snarling, vicious wolves.

She knew that her father had hoped to get her acclimated to shooting animals, wanting to make sure she would always be safe because animals could turn on her in a heartbeat, he'd explained, but she never did.

Eventually, her father began to drink more and more, and those Sunday afternoons in the woods, shooting at the pictures he'd posted for her, became a thing of the past. But she never forgot how to shoot and, on occasion, still went out to practice on her own. With Grayson and his cronies spreading their scourge here, who knew when that ability—to hit whatever she aimed for—might just come in handy?

Reaching the front window, she got there just in time to see Hawk pulling up.

The smile on her lips spread all through her. He was here!

She was about to hurry to the door to open it when a light in the distance caught her eye. It took her less than half a second to realize that it was actually two lights, not one. Two, like the headlights of an approaching vehicle.

Had Hawk brought someone with him?

But if he had, why weren't they both traveling in his car? And why was he now getting out of his vehicle without so much as a backward glance at the other car? It was as if he had no idea that there *was* another car approaching in the distance.

Nerves stretched taut began to dance through her. She had come to realize that she had grown to be a great deal less trusting than she had once been.

Backing away from the front window, Carly hurried over to the gun rack, the phrase *better safe than sorry* drumming through her head.

The last thing she wanted was to be sorry.

She had just unlocked the chain that she kept threaded through the weapons when she heard it.

A sound pealing like the crack of thunder.

Except that it wasn't thunder. She'd heard it often enough to know the difference between distant thunder and a gunshot.

There was no hesitation.

Grabbing the rifle closest to her, Carly hurried back to the front door. With no children in the house to worry about, she knew the weapon in her hand was fully loaded and ready to be discharged.

Carly threw open the door, then got her weapon ready, just in time to fire at whoever was firing a second shot at Hawk. Carly returned fire even before she realized that Hawk was down, obviously hit by that first shot she'd heard.

Rushing out to him, her heart pounding madly, Carly kept firing in the general direction of her quarry. She was intent on providing cover for herself and, more importantly, for Hawk, who she now realized was bleeding profusely from his left arm.

"Can you walk?" she cried, her eyes trained on the now-retreating back of the man who had followed Hawk here and tried to kill him. "Hawk, can you hear me?" she all but shouted when he didn't answer her. She didn't allow herself even to contemplate the reason why he wouldn't answer her.

"Yeah," Hawk managed to bite off, swallowing most of a string of curses. His arm felt as if it was on fire.

He should have seen that coming, Hawk angrily upbraided himself. But he'd been so preoccupied with the thought of seeing Carly, the thought of *being* with Carly, that he had let his guard slip. He hadn't been as careful as he should have been. And worst of all, he hadn't realized that he had a tail following him.

What a damn stupid rookie mistake, he thought angrily. He should have never allowed this to happen.

Carly was suddenly beside him, down on one knee as she kept shooting, providing their cover fire.

"Here!" she ordered, presenting her shoulder to him. "Lean on me."

Before he realized what she was doing, Carly had her shoulder wedged under his. With one massive effort, she struggled to bring him up to his feet. He did what he could to make it easier, willing himself to be stronger.

Their shadows fused together to appear as one wide, awkward creature, Hawk and Carly made their way quickly into the house, never turning their back on the shooter, even though it looked as though he'd given up and was fleeing.

The moment she had Hawk inside the house, Carly quickly slammed the front door and bolted it. Only then, with her arm wrapped around his middle now, did she half walk, half drag Hawk over to the sofa.

"Here, lie down on the couch," she ordered, all but dropping him there as she released the heavy weight of his frame from her aching shoulders. There was blood all over one side of her. "I'm checking the other windows and doors to make sure we don't get any uninvited pests slithering in."

As good as her word, Carly quickly and methodically checked each and every window, testing its integrity just to make sure it held. She also made sure that the back door was still secure.

"What was that all about?" she asked, raising her voice so that Hawk could hear her.

"Had to be one of Grayson's men," Hawk guessed. He closed his eyes for a moment, gathering his strength to him. The bullet was still lodged in his shoulder, and it had to come out. If they went to the nearest hospital in the next town, he might bleed out before they got there. And there was no way he could go to the Urgent Care Center in Cold Plains. He'd be dead before morning.

No, this was something that Carly was going to have to do. He wondered if she was up to it, or if, ultimately, she'd be too squeamish.

The woman who had come running to his rescue without a thought for her own safety had been magnificent—and not even remotely acquainted with the term *squeamish*.

"I think he feels that I'm getting close to something, although damned if I know what," he speculated. There was no other reason for the man to want to kill him, he thought. And he was sure that Grayson was behind this attack. As sure as he was that the sun was coming up tomorrow.

"He just doesn't want you nosing around, asking questions. It undermines his authority and his hold on 'his' people," Carly called back.

Satisfied that the windows were as secure as she could get them, Carly hurried back to the living room. It suddenly occurred to her, a second before she reached the living room, that by rushing to Hawk's aid, she had blown her cover.

She couldn't go back to the community center to try to see Mia. After she had just fired on one of his men, there was no doubt in her mind that Grayson would kill her if he saw her.

She didn't regret it. In her heart, she knew that if she hadn't been there, or if she'd hesitated and played it safe,

Hawk would be lying dead in her front yard—instead of bleeding on her sofa.

Getting him patched up was all that mattered, she told herself as she hurried over to him.

"Did the bullet go through?" she asked even as she gently began to examine the wound herself. There was no through and through, which could only mean one thing, she thought, her stomach sinking as she heard Hawk answer her question.

"No," he told her, "I think it's still in there." Looking up at her, he said, "You know what you have to do."

Throw up comes to mind, Carly thought, doing her best not to turn a very sickly shade of green.

Chapter 14

This was no time to think about herself, Carly silently chided. There were a number of different possibilities if the bullet was left where it was, none of them good. Besides, it wasn't as if she'd never seen a wound up close before, or cleaned one for that matter. It had just never involved someone she loved the way she loved Hawk.

"You're going to need some alcohol, bandages, a needle and thread—and your sharpest knife," Hawk said from the kitchen chair she'd helped move him to, trying his best to focus on details and not the sharp pain. The amount of blood he'd lost was making him feel light-headed, and he needed to remain conscious so that he could help Carly. He really should go to a hospital but he didn't trust anyone, and for this case, he had to fly under the radar.

She had already returned to the kitchen from the

bathroom, her arms filled with the items he had just rattled off.

"I know," she said, depositing them one by one on the kitchen table, lining them up in front of him. "I've done this before."

He looked at her in surprise. "When?" he asked.

It wasn't one of her fonder memories and up until now, she'd kept it to herself. "Dad and his friend used to go out hunting with enough alcohol in them to stock a small liquor store."

That was after her father had decided that drinking and hunting with his buddies was a lot more fun than going out for target practice with a little girl, she remembered. There was a time when that realization had pinched her stomach and made a sadness descend over her. But that time had long since passed. Now whenever she thought of her late father or anything associated with him, she felt nothing. She was completely removed from that period of her life. It no longer mattered.

"One time his friends came back carrying Dad between them—not exactly an easy feat since they were all falling-down drunk. Seems that one of the guys had accidentally mistaken him for a deer when he was in the bushes, relieving himself, and shot Dad. There was no time to take him to the next town to see a doctor, so I was drafted."

Hawk frowned. She couldn't have been that old. "Why not one of the other men?" he asked.

That would have probably hastened her father's demise. "Would you want someone trying to remove a bullet out of you when their hand was as steady as an earthquake?" To emphasize her point, she held out her hand and showed him how badly the men's hands had shaken.

He saw the point. "Guess not."

She went over to the sink and poured the rubbing alcohol liberally over the knife, disinfecting it. "Well, neither did my dad. He wasn't *that* drunk. So I was elected."

He wondered why she'd never told him about this before. What else hadn't she told him about? At one point he would have sworn that they had told each other everything. Everything because they had so much in common and had come together, seeking solace and comfort in the fact that the other *knew* exactly what they were going through, having an irrational drunk as a father. Now he was no longer so sure.

"Just how old were you?" he asked.

She didn't even have to think about it. "Almost eleven. It was the year after my mother died," she added in a quieter voice. There were times when she caught herself still missing her mother. That was never the case with her father. He had died *years* after he'd been lost to her.

Checking everything she'd laid out on the table, she said, "I need one more thing before I get started." With that, Carly hurried out of the room.

He looked at the items on the table. "What else do you need?" he called out, curious.

"Technically, I don't need it. But you do," she told him as she walked back into the room.

She placed an old bottle of whiskey on the table right

in front of him. The bottle was dusty. It was also un-opened. He glanced at her sharply. If asked, he would have easily bet that there was no liquor in the house. Obviously he would have lost that bet.

"What are you doing with that?" he asked.

Grabbing a kitchen towel, she quickly cleaned the dust on the bottle. She tossed the towel onto the back of a chair, removed the bottle's cap and set it to the side.

"This is the last bottle my father bought. He dropped dead of a heart attack just as he started to open it. I'm not exactly sure why I've kept it all these years, but now I'm glad I did. It's not going to knock you out," she told him, getting a glass from the cupboard, "but at least it might help you put up with the pain a little." Saying that, she poured a liberal amount of the amber liquid into a glass, then held it out to him. "Here."

Maybe it might help, he thought as he accepted the offered glass. Rather than just sip the drink slowly, as was his habit if he drank at all, Hawk tilted the glass back and drank down the contents quickly, draining it. He put it back down on the table with a "thwack" that resounded through the room.

The whiskey dulled his senses, dragging a fire through his belly and his limbs. He was still having trouble focusing, but now he didn't mind as much.

"Have at it," he told her, shifting in his chair so that his injured shoulder now faced her. "I'm ready, Dr. Finn," he declared, deliberately emphasizing the title she had no claim to.

Well, he might be ready, she thought, but she really wasn't. Still, this needed to be done, and the longer she delayed, the worse the consequences might be for Hawk. She brought the knife over to the sink and repeated the ritual of liberally pouring the last of the rubbing alcohol over both sides of it. And while she was doing that, she also did one more thing.

"Your lips are moving," Hawk noticed. "But I don't hear anything."

"You're not supposed to." That was her answer, but he was obviously waiting for more, so she explained very quietly, "I'm praying."

The admission surprised him. He thought for a moment, then found that between the triple shot of whiskey he'd just consumed and the blood he'd lost, he really couldn't do that well.

"Didn't know you did that," he told her.

Carly took a deep breath. The rubbing alcohol was all gone and, with it, her excuse for stalling. She was ready, whether or not God was.

"On occasion," she answered, then nodded at the bottle on the table. "Want another drink before we get started?"

"I'm good," Hawk told her, bracing himself. He had no intention of passing out like his old man had habitually done. Drinking himself into a stupor was his father's usual way of operating. "Go ahead."

Oh God, was all Carly could think, over and over again, as she applied the point of her knife to Hawk's flesh and began to go in. Although she knew that this wasn't his fault, she found that digging for the bullet was exceedingly difficult. For one thing, the muscles in Hawk's arm were as hard as rocks. Pushing the knife into his flesh was far easier in theory than in actual practice.

Amazingly, Hawk wasn't making any noise. Muscles or not, this *had* to hurt. "You all right?" she asked, slanting an uneasy glance at him.

"I've been better," he answered through solidly clenched teeth.

She didn't want to hurt him like this, but she had no other choice. "I'm sorry—"

"Just find it," he ordered, doing his best not to snap at her.

"I can't," she cried, growing more frustrated the deeper she probed for the bullet.

And then, finally, she felt it, felt a definite resistance of another kind. The point of her knife had touched metal.

"I think I found it."

Thank God, he silently cried. Out loud he merely muttered, "Good for you."

"Just a little longer," she promised, hoping she wasn't lying as she angled the knife in her hand, trying to get under the bullet to move it along.

And then, in what felt like a million light-years later, she finally managed to get it out. Such a little thing, causing so much damage, she couldn't help thinking as she put it on the table.

But there was no time to take a breath or admire her handiwork. Without anything to hold it back, Hawk's blood began to flow freely from the hole in his arm. Acting fast, Carly jammed a large wad of cotton against the wound, temporarily stemming the flow until she could reach for her needle. Her stomach, in turmoil, all but rose up into her mouth.

She felt sick. Whether with relief or the thought of what *could* have happened, she wasn't sure. But the one thing she knew was that she wanted desperately just to throw up.

As if sensing what she was going through, Hawk said in a very soothing voice, "You're doing just fine, Carly. Better than I could have hoped."

"I bet you say that to all the women who stitch you up," she quipped, releasing a huge sigh. There were at least half a dozen sighs just like that inside of her, waiting for release.

"Believe it or not, this is the first time I've ever been shot." He'd gone nine years with the Bureau without incident. He couldn't say that about himself anymore.

Something didn't make sense to her. "Then how did you know what I'd need to use?"

He supposed that was a valid question. "It's not the first time I've been around a bullet wound, just the first time I was the one on the receiving end," he clarified.

"Oh."

A sense of triumph suddenly hit her. She'd done it. She'd gotten the bullet out, cleaned the wound and sewn it up to prevent it from bleeding. He was going to make it. The relief continued to flower within her.

She took a large gauze pad, opened it and placed the white square on the wound she'd just closed. She then secured it in place with strips of tape around the perimeter of the gauze. That done, she sat back to look at her handiwork.

"I'm done," she announced with no small pleasure in her voice.

"Nice work," he commended. After making a quick call to his crew to make sure everything was okay there, he leaned heavily on his good arm and pushed himself up on his feet.

She was instantly alert and on hers. "Where are you going?" she asked.

This wasn't the time to sit back and take it easy. Good men lost their lives that way, he recalled. "To look around outside and make sure that the guy who shot me isn't coming back to finish the job."

"Only place you're going is to bed, mister," she informed him, sounding more stern than he could ever recall hearing her. "I can check to make sure that coward hasn't come back."

"I'm not going to bed," he told her firmly.

She knew that tone, knew there was no arguing with it. She compromised. "Okay, then sack out on the sofa if that suits you better. You've got a clear view of the front door as well as the window that way," she pointed out. "But you are not going outside, understood?" she said in a firm, take-no-prisoners voice.

If he'd had more strength, he would have argued with her. But as it was, he really didn't have the wherewithal to conduct an argument. He just was not in control the way he normally was. Between the blood loss and the quickly consumed alcohol, which had gone straight to his head, he felt as if the room insisted on making a circular journey, and it seemed to be spinning more and more quickly.

"Understood," he murmured, surrendering. "Did you get a look at him?" he asked her as, with her help, he made his way unsteadily to the couch. Somehow, the distance had become farther than he remembered.

"Yes, at the very last minute," she told him. And when she recognized the sniper, it was both a shock— and quite honestly—something she'd half expected. "The guy who shot you was Grayson's pretty boy, Charlie Rhodes." She set her mouth grimly as she told Hawk, "He's going to be best man at Mia's wedding." It was the startling contrast of blond hair against the dark night that had triggered recognition for her.

All but collapsing onto the sofa, Hawk looked up at her. His brain was foggy, but he struggled to make sense of what he was being told. Rhodes had clearly seen her coming to help him. It was because of her that he was still alive. That meant that, in Rhodes's eyes, she was a traitor.

Rhodes would go straight to Grayson with that. There was no reason not to. And he knew the consequences.

"The wedding," Hawk echoed. "How are you going to stop it?"

"Now that they know I'm not one of them?" Was this what he was asking her? The answer was heartbreakingly simple. "I'm not. Grayson is never going to allow me to get anywhere near my sister after what happened here tonight." Had she been as brainwashed as Grayson had believed her to be, she would have never even been seeing Hawk, much less coming to his rescue by firing at a member of his handpicked circle of associates.

Even exhausted and weak, Hawk knew how huge a sacrifice Carly had just made to save him. "I'm sorry, Carly."

She forced a smile to her lips, trying to appear as if she'd made her peace. "Not your fault."

But it was, and he knew it. If he hadn't turned up, she wouldn't have had to choose between coming to his rescue or saving her sister. He had to make it up to her. He began to say as much, but discovered to his confusion, that the words just weren't coming out. Not only that, but his thoughts now moved aimlessly about in his head in slow motion, like disoriented puffs of cotton at the mercy of the hot summer breeze.

Hawk couldn't think clearly.

He would have to wait to tell her.

Later, he'd tell her later.

It was the last thought that drifted through his head before his eyes slid closed.

With a sudden, jolting start that played along the length of his entire body, Hawk woke up. Initial disorientation dissolved in increments. There was a blanket partially covering him, the bottom half pooling onto the floor. Daylight forcefully pushed its way into the farmhouse through the bay window. Hawk drew in a deep breath, trying to clear his head.

How long had he been asleep?

Sitting up, he saw that he wasn't alone in the room, the way he'd first thought. Carly was propped up in the dilapidated armchair, her rifle laying across her thighs, giving every appearance of being ready to be pressed into service at a moment's notice.

She was awake and, unlike him, gave no sign that this was a recent event. When he blinked and looked closer, he realized that she looked tired. Like someone who had been up all night.

Again, that was his fault.

"How long have you been sitting there?" he asked.

The tension that had built up in her neck was practically killing her. She tried to rotate her shoulders to alleviate it a little. It didn't help. "All night," she told him.

Guilt burrowed through him and grew. He was the professional here. He was the one who was supposed to be protecting her, not the other way around. "Did you get any sleep?"

"Sleep's highly overrated," she answered flippantly, then added more honestly, "I thought it would be safer if one of us stayed awake, just in case." She saw the concern that passed over his chiseled features, and it touched her that he cared. "I can catch up on my sleep some other time," she assured him. "Right now, I wanted to be sure Charlie didn't decide to pay us another little visit, maybe this time bringing along some of his little friends to finish what he started."

Thinking about it—since she'd had nothing to do all night but watch Hawk sleep, listen for strange sounds and think—it had occurred to her that Grayson's baby-faced disciple surrounded himself with men who seemed downright dangerous.

She put nothing past that crew, including torture,

rape and murder. "The last thing I wanted was for us to be caught by surprise by those happy henchmen."

Carly got up from the armchair, leaning her rifle against it. She watched Hawk with concern. He'd moaned several times during the night, no doubt due to pain, but mercifully, he'd gone on sleeping.

"How's the arm?" she asked.

Right now, it felt pretty stiff and ached like hell. "This wouldn't be the time to take up juggling," he cracked. "But all things considered, it's pretty good," he pronounced, looking at it as if it had just caught his attention. And then he glanced back at her, a grin slowly curving his lips. "You're welcome to stitch me up anytime."

That was one task she didn't ever want to repeat. She'd prefer her stitching to be relegated to mending clothes.

"Don't take this the wrong way, but I'll pass," she told him. "I'm going to make some coffee. You interested?"

"Always," he said, his voice low. And then he added, "And I'd like some coffee, too."

That stopped her cold in her tracks for a good minute. Turning slowly, she looked at Hawk. Their eyes met and held for what seemed like forever. Hawk smiled at her as he began to get up again.

Snapping out of her momentary mental revelry, a revelry that took her to places she told herself he *couldn't* have meant for her to go—there had to be some other kind of meaning behind his words than the one that had instantly popped up in her mind—she said in a loud, authoritative voice, "Sit."

Hawk remained standing, though for the moment, he leaned his hand on the back of the sofa for subtle support. "That might work on your dog, Carly," he began on a warning note. He had always *hated* being ordered around, and she knew it.

"Don't have a dog," she pointed out glibly.

"I don't wonder," he said, taking small steps, each one a little more steady than the last. He was getting his sea legs back, he thought sarcastically. "Any dog of yours would have to run away from home to regain his self-respect." Switching gears, he told her, "I'll 'sit' in the kitchen. Will that make you happy?"

What would have made her happy was if she could have gone back and relived her life, this time making sure not to make the same mistakes that would have brought her to this point.

But there was no point in wishing for what hadn't a chance in hell of coming true. She had to deal with what was in front of her. She always had, and she didn't intend to change now.

So she pretended not to care one way or another and shrugged at what he'd just said. "What you do is entirely up to you."

"Good to know we're on the same page," he replied, a trace of humor in his voice as well as his eyes.

What he needed to do right now was to build up his strength and endurance. He approached the kitchen table, reminding himself of all he had to do. He had another twenty-four hours to get ready—and that included getting his body back to working at, if not maximum efficiency, then at least, an acceptable level.

Carly had risked everything she held dear to save him. He intended to pay her back for that. It was the least he could do.

Chapter 15

They were cutting it so close to the actual time of the ceremony, Carly felt she could barely breathe.

But they had to cut it this close, Hawk had explained to her, and she both understood and fully agreed. Understood that their biggest asset here was the element of surprise, and the timetable for that had to be precise. Since the front door was no longer a viable option, she and Hawk would be gaining access to the community center from within, via an old, long-unused underground route.

She'd all but forgotten that it even existed.

There was an old network of underground passages threading their way beneath the various buildings erected in Cold Plains. Since none of the passages were remotely straightforward and had been dug almost two hundred years ago, not many were aware of their existence, and the few who were had no occasion to mention them.

But Carly did.

She suddenly remembered the stories her mother had told her years ago, passed on from her grandfather, about how the tunnels were initially dug to protect the early Wyoming settlers from the wrath of outraged Native Americans looking to rid their land of the scourge that had oppressed them: the pioneers who were settling all over their precious land.

"And I know that there's one right under the community center," Carly had told Hawk yesterday as they were trying to come up with a way to rescue Mia from what Carly considered a fate worse than death. "It comes up right into the old storage room at the back of the building."

"Great." That gave them a way into the community center, but that still left the little matter of getting into the tunnel to begin with. "Do you know where that particular tunnel starts?"

Carly did her best to remember. Vague fragments, mosaic pieces from her childhood, tumbled about in her mind, like a kaleidoscope, at first refusing to come together to form any whole.

She concentrated harder, refusing to give up and eventually, it came to her. "One of the ways into the tunnels was this old, abandoned mine shaft right outside of town."

That sounded vaguely familiar to him, like something he'd seen when he was a kid here. "They struck a vein of silver back at the turn of the last century," he recalled abruptly. It surprised him how easily memories from his childhood came back to him, despite all his efforts to block that part of his life—both man and boy here in Cold Plains—from his mind.

But then, he reminded himself, he'd never forgotten a single thing about Carly, and she was a huge part of that time.

She nodded. Tales of the silver mine were as close to a legend as they had in this little town—before Grayson and his crew came.

"I think I remember my mother saying that the mine stayed open almost twenty years before it was boarded up. People kept hoping to find another mother lode, but all they ever got were just a couple of small veins that wound up petering out."

"We played there as kids." At the time, he'd never thought to go much farther than the mouth. It was during a period of his childhood when ghosts had held a real threat for him.

Hawk paused now, thinking about what might be ahead. Taking Carly along was just putting her life in jeopardy. "Listen, Carly, this could get really dangerous."

They were already in his car, ready to leave. "What's your point? I already know that."

He shifted in his seat to look at her. "Maybe what you don't know is that I don't want to risk you getting hurt."

Then don't leave when this is all over, she thought. Annoyed with herself and her moment of weakness at a time like this, she pushed the thought aside. "It's my sister we're rescuing. If anything you should be the one staying behind." She gazed at the makeshift sling she'd insisted he use. "You've only got one good arm."

"One's all it takes," he assured her. One hand to aim and shoot.

Hawk took out his cell phone and glanced at the screen. For once, the indicator said he was receiving a decent signal. He'd already gotten in touch with Jeffers, Patterson and Rosenbloom yesterday, instructing the agents to get a SWAT detail out as quickly as possible from Cheyenne because they were going in to take down a potential killer. He even had the excuse covered for going in: it had conveniently been provided for him by Charlie Rhodes. Since Carly had identified Grayson's second in command as the man who had tried to kill him, they were coming to arrest him, wedding ceremony or no wedding ceremony. Attempting to kill a federal agent was not a crime to be lightly shrugged off with a slap on the wrists. If convicted—and why wouldn't he be?—Charlie could be facing a great many years in prison.

With backup alerted, all that was left was to execute the main plan—which hinged heavily on gaining access to the center from within.

"You sure I can't talk you into holding down the fort here?" he asked one final time. He really did have enough on his mind without adding someone else to worry about to it.

There was no reason to "hold down" anything and they both knew it. Anyone who was anyone would be attending this wedding—at Grayson's behest. And no one crossed Samuel Grayson.

In response to his query, Carly gave him a long, penetrating look, which felt as if it went clear down to his bones. "What do you think?"

"I think I'd feel better if I had eyes in the back of my head, because I really don't like taking you into the thick of things like this," he said, setting his mouth hard as he stared out through the windshield for a moment. He didn't like the idea of actually bringing her to a potential crime scene. A crime scene, ironically, that had yet to become one.

"You're not 'taking' me anywhere," she informed him as they finally started heading to the cave. "If anything, I'm taking you," she pointed out. "I'm the one who remembered the tunnels and knows how to get to them."

There really was no point in arguing. He would lose, and it was just a waste of time. "I keep forgetting how damn stubborn you are," he said under his breath. The statement was accompanied by not-quite-silent grumbling.

"I like the word *resourceful* better," she informed him.

Potato, po-tot-toe, he was still not happy about having her come along with him.

They arrived at the mine shaft in a short amount of time.

Carly was right, he thought. She knew every shortcut in this underdeveloped region. Armed with flashlights, they went in. Hawk insisted on going in first.

This way, if there was trouble, he'd be the first to know. That left her room to escape—as if she would even try. Carly had already proved that she was the type to stand shoulder to shoulder with someone she cared about, not flee at the first sign of trouble.

It was, Carly thought at one point, like moving through the bowels of hell. The area was stuffy, dark except for the twin, thin beams of light cast by their separate flashlights. She just *knew* they were sharing the crammed space with umpteen rodents, which could come swarming around them at any moment.

She'd had great affection for all animals, big and small. But when it came to rats, she and the animal kingdom parted company. Rats made her flesh creep.

A little like the way Grayson did, she now thought. How could that man hold so many people under his thumb? It had to be some kind of aberration of nature.

They continued walking.

An uneasiness began to grow as she started thinking that perhaps she hadn't been right, that the mine shaft just led farther and farther into the mine and not into the center of town. Just when she was about to voice her concern to Hawk, suggest that they turn back, she heard a strange, thundering noise echoing overhead.

She looked at Hawk, a question in her eyes.

"Sounds like footsteps to me," he acknowledged. "Lots of footsteps." He let out the breath he'd been holding. "I think we've arrived, Columbus. Have to admit I had my doubts there for a while."

The man was nothing if not honest. And she hadn't

been when she sent him away, she thought as the guilt flared inside her.

"You weren't the only one," she murmured more to herself than to him.

Light was seeping in up ahead, coming in where the storage room door didn't quite meet its frame. She was about to open it when he put his hand up, silently cautioning her to stay where she was. He might not be able to talk her out of coming, but at the very least, if for some reason they wound up walking into a trap, then he wanted to be the first one to go down, not her. It would buy her enough time to get away.

Not that he was about to say any of this to her, because it would only result in yet another argument. The woman just didn't know the meaning of the words *staying safe*. But he intended to teach her—if it was the last thing he ever did.

Reaching the door, he turned the doorknob ever so slowly and eased the door open. They were in a storage room all right. It appeared to be a catchall for discarded items that had lived out their usefulness from the various rooms and offices. Apparently someone didn't seem to have the heart to throw them out just yet.

That was how pack rats got started, he thought. As for him, he was a minimalist. The less he owned, the less those things owned him. Turning, he beckoned for Carly to follow him—not that he actually had to. She'd seemed practically one step ahead of him all morning.

The hallway looked clear, so they advanced, making their way to the room where the ceremony was about to take place.

As they turned a corner, they surprised one of Grayson's henchmen—obviously playing the part of a groomsman/guard. Momentarily getting the drop on the man, Hawk acted swiftly, grabbing him by the head and twisting it—hard. Fresh pain shot through his bandaged shoulder.

There was a sickening snap.

Carly didn't ask if the man was dead. She knew. When Hawk released him, the guard fell bonelessly to the floor.

Carly waited a second, thinking that a surge of remorse would overcome her at any moment but it didn't materialize. These were the people who had come in and stripped her friends and neighbors—her *sister*— of not just their worldly possessions and their integrity but their very souls. She felt nothing about eliminating them before they had a chance to do the same to people she cared about. Death here was the great equalizer, not unlike the weapon she still carried with her.

"You okay?" Hawk asked, his eyes sweeping over her face.

"Don't worry about me," she told him, waving him on. "We've got a wedding to stop."

It seemed almost like poetic justice that the words, "If anyone knows why these two should not wed, speak now—" were the ones being said just as Hawk pushed open the doors, causing everything to come to a stunned, crashing halt.

"Everybody freeze," Hawk ordered. "I'm a federal agent!"

"I do," Carly cried, addressing Grayson who, under

the guise of "minister," was performing the ceremony. "I object."

She noted the angry look on her sister's face a second before she heard Grayson whisper something to the best man. Color drained from Mia's face. She'd heard what was being said.

The next moment, as if in slow motion, Carly saw Charlie Rhodes pull a gun from beneath his tuxedo jacket—he'd apparently tucked it into the back of his waistband, she realized—and fire in her direction.

She heard Mia scream her name just as she slammed against the floor. Not because she'd been hit but because Hawk had thrown himself over her, protecting her with his own body as he pushed her out of the line of fire.

"Told you to say behind!" he bit off as he rolled forward to return fire. Charlie hadn't been the only one who had brought a gun to the ceremony.

It still might have gone very badly for them, Hawk reflected later, had he not thought to "invite" his own "guests" to the wedding.

Just as the gunfire began being exchanged, the doors on the other side of the room burst open and Rosenbloom, Patterson and Jeffers, along with several other FBI agents, all wearing Kevlar vests, took over the room.

"Nobody move!" Hawk ordered again, getting up from the floor. This time, caught between two lines of fire, everyone obeyed. Hawk paused, his eyes and weapon trained on Grayson as he extended his hand to Carly.

Wrapping her fingers around his hand, Carly rose to her feet.

"You all right?" he asked.

She was bruised where she'd hit the floor, but she wasn't complaining. All things considered, she'd gotten off lucky. "Never better."

"Carly! Carly, did he—did Charlie—did Charlie shoot you?" Mia cried almost hysterically. Her arms filled with taffeta and organza, her sister came rushing over to her as fast as she could. Her face was still as pale as her wedding dress. "He tried to kill you," she said, stunned and clearly very shaken by what she'd just been forced to witness.

"Not exactly a quality one wants in their best man," Carly quipped. She wrapped one arm around Mia and hugged her. That was when she realized that Mia was trembling. "Are *you* all right?" she asked, even as more agents kept coming in, surrounding the wedding guests and ordering everyone over to a corner of the banquet room.

"I don't know," Mia answered honestly. She seemed dazed and confused as she looked up to meet her sister's eyes. "I thought everything here was finally so perfect. That my life was going to be so perfect." A bottomless sadness became evident in her voice. "He was going to kill you," she repeated numbly.

It was unclear if she meant Charlie or Grayson, but now wasn't the time to ask. It was enough that Mia finally understood that there was a viciousness here that threatened her very existence.

"I know," Carly replied quietly, keeping her voice at a calm, soothing level.

Mia appeared to sink further into her confusion and feelings of remorse and depression. "You came to save me, didn't you?"

"I told Mom I'd take care of you," she reminded her younger sister. "This was part of that promise."

She looked at Mia, trying to get a handle on what was going on in the younger girl's mind. Mia looked as if she was very close to a breakdown. And why not? Paradise had just blown up in her face.

Her sister would need help processing all this and coping with it, Carly thought. Grayson had done a number on Mia's head. It would take someone professional, versed in deprogramming, to bring her sister around with a minimum of consequences, she decided with regret.

But at least they'd gotten her out of Grayson's clutches. And Mia hadn't married Carrington. All in all, this was a very good day, Carly silently congratulated herself.

"Why don't we get you out of that dress and into something a little more comfortable?" she suggested to her sister.

Mia stared down as if she wasn't sure what she was wearing. "There's blood on it," she murmured, noticing the thin line of red across the bodice. "Is it Charlie's?" she asked.

Acting quickly, Hawk had brought the baby-faced man down with a single shot. Carly pressed her lips together and nodded. "Yes."

"Good," Mia said with feeling, then quickly raised her eyes to Carly's before lowering them again.

Maybe more than a little help, Carly thought. Her sister appeared as if she was retreating into a shell.

Looking around, Carly saw the agent Hawk had introduced to her as Tom Jeffers nearby, and she called him over now. When he crossed to her, asking if he could do something for her, she turned Mia over to him.

"Could you please take my sister back to her room?" she requested. "She needs to get out of those clothes."

About to protest that this wasn't part of what he was doing right now, Jeffers took one look at the distraught young face and changed his mind.

"Sure." Jeffers put his elbow out in an exaggerated fashion, indicating that Mia should take it for support. She looked as if she needed it. "Why don't you show me where it is?" he coaxed.

Mia nodded. "It's upstairs," she told him. The agent very gently led her away.

With Mia taken care of for the moment, Carly searched for Hawk. She finally saw him talking with several other agents. He was clearly the one in charge, and she felt a sense of pride watching him. Her initial instinct to make the supreme sacrifice and send him away had been the right move to make after all. Hawk was very much in his element here. This was where he belonged, leading people who ultimately made a difference and took pride in doing it.

Hawk was born to be what he was, a special agent with the FBI.

Drawing closer, she immediately recognized one of the men.

Ford McCall wasn't one of Hawk's people, he was from around here. A local deputy. One who, she now realized after she'd heard him making several arrests, was not corrupt the way that the police chief, Fargo, clearly was. The latter belonged to Grayson. Ford was obviously his own man. Thank God.

Nodding at Ford now, she turned toward Hawk. "How's your arm?" she wanted to know.

"Aches, but I'm still standing." And after what had just taken place in the past half hour, that was definitely an accomplishment.

As she looked around, it occurred to Carly that Grayson was nowhere in sight. Had he left? Or better yet, had he gone down in the cross fire? "Are you arresting Grayson?" she asked.

A frustrated expression came into his eyes as he did his best not to change his expression. "Right now, we don't have anything that'll stick."

She looked at him, stunned. "But he's behind all this," she cried. "Behind the murders. Maybe he's even had Susannah killed," she said, thinking about the conversation she'd had with Samuel the other day.

"Believe me, I'm not part of the man's fan club, either. I'd take him down in a heartbeat, if I could," Hawk told her. "He probably had his own brother killed. It wouldn't be the first time one twin murdered the other," he added grimly.

There'd still been no word from Micah. As soon as he got finished here, he would personally hire a private investigator to try to locate the missing would-be informant. He still firmly believed that Micah wouldn't have called him, then just vanished without a word.

Hawk surprised her by changing his tone of voice and looking directly at her as he said, "Looks like I've got a lot to keep me here in Cold Plains."

Was he saying more than she thought he was saying? "For how long?" she asked.

He spread his hands wide. "Right now, it's open-ended. I'm still trying to find out who killed those women and why. Jane Doe's identity is still a mystery, Grayson's brother is still missing—"

"Don't forget Susannah Paul and her baby. They couldn't have just disappeared like that," she reminded him.

"Right, there's that, too," he agreed. Drawing her over to an empty corner, Hawk lowered his voice as he continued talking. "Samuel Grayson is the key to all of this, and I'm not going anywhere until I find out just how he's connected. And when I find out, I intend to take him down."

She liked the sound of that. But she liked something else more. "So I guess I'll be seeing you for a while."

"I guess so."

Looking away for a second, Hawk blew out a breath. He was playing it safe again. Damn it, he was tired of playing it safe. He hadn't played it safe earlier when he'd put himself between Carly and the bullet meant for her. Somewhere, on some invisible tally, he was certain that he was running out of second chances, so he had better take advantage of this one before his luck ran out completely.

"Especially if you marry me," Hawk said to her out of the blue.

It was a minor accomplishment that she'd kept her jaw from dropping like a brick. It took her a good, long second to collect herself. When she did, she stared at him.

"Did you just say—"

"Yes," he answered, cutting her off.

No, not this time. This time, the *I*s were going to be dotted and the *T*s were going to be crossed. Just this once, their abilities to end each other's sentences wouldn't cut it.

She needed this spelled out.

"Let me finish," she insisted. "Did you—" She stopped abruptly as she pressed her lips together. Her mouth had suddenly gone dry mid-word. Regrouping, she tried again. "I think my hearing's going, because I thought I just heard you ask me to marry you."

He grinned at her, amusement dancing in his eyes. "Well, if your hearing's going, maybe I'd better reconsider my question. But for the record, yes, I did ask you to marry me."

"Why?"

"Why did I ask?"

"Yes." She nodded for emphasis. "Why did you ask?"

He thought a moment. "Because dragging you by the hair to my cave isn't the way it's done anymore." Before she could comment on his Neanderthal reference, he took her hand in his and became very serious. "I got a second chance when I wound up coming back here. And another second chance when you saved my life the other night. The way I see it, whoever's in charge of handing out second chances is going to think they're being wasted on me, and I'll be left out in the cold. I don't want to be in the cold anymore," he told her sincerely. "I want to be with you. If that means spending the rest of my life as a farmer in this two-bit town, I'll adjust."

"No way," she told him adamantly. "I like the idea of my husband being an FBI special agent." She smiled and succeeded in lighting up his entire life. "It has a nice ring to it."

"Your husband," he repeated, savoring the way that sounded.

She watched his face, trying to get a handle on what he was thinking as she answered, "That's what I said."

He raised his eyebrows hopefully. "Then your answer is yes?"

For once in her life, she wasn't going to be straightforward. For once, just **once**, she was going to be cagey. "Depends on the question."

Now he *really* didn't understand. "But I just asked you—"

"No, you didn't," she pointed out. "You mentioned it. In passing. You *didn't* ask." She turned her face up to his. "A woman likes to be asked. Formally."

He could understand that. "All right." He took her hand. "Carly Finn, I'm tired of feeling as if something's missing. I'm tired of missing you," he said with feeling. "Will you marry me and make me whole again?"

She slid her arms up around his neck, and he held her

to him with his one good arm. Her eyes danced. This was fun, and she savored her moment. "What do you think?"

"I've learned not to second-guess anything," he answered honestly.

"Okay," she said. Tilting her head up, she told him, "Then read my lips." Before he could pretend to look at them closer, she rose up on her toes and pressed her mouth against his.

Hawk had his answer.

He made the most of it.

Epilogue

"You're so much more of a beautiful bride than I was—or almost was," Mia amended as she fussed over Carly's train. She wanted to make sure that when her sister walked out onto the newly constructed patio that Hawk's FBI friends had just finished working on three days ago, the appliqué on the material wouldn't bunch up or accidentally snag.

"What are you talking about?" Carly cried loyally. "You were a gorgeous bride—despite the horrible circumstances."

Determined to make her point, Mia angled the tri-winged mirror on the wall over the bureau so that her older sister could get an actual good look at herself. Satisfied that the lighting was just right, she gestured toward the mirror while standing behind her sister.

"Look," she ordered. "You're positively glowing. I

didn't have that really happy glow. I just had a hazy look on my face," she recalled. There was no remorse, no regret. It was an episode in her past, and it was over. She was moving forward. That was the lesson she'd taken away from her weeks in the deprogramming center. "I can't believe what I almost did," she admitted, shaking her head. The only remorse she felt was for what Carly had had to put up with.

"I'm sorry for what I put you through," she said honestly. Then her apology broadened. "And I'm really sorry I didn't have enough time to get you a wedding present."

Carly turned away from the mirror and looked at her sister, her eyes brimming with love—and a few tears. "Having you back, just being you, is the best present I could possibly ask for," she assured Mia.

Mia had just arrived very early this morning, having completed her stint at the deprogramming facility that Hawk had found for her. It had been an intense, accelerated program, done at Hawk's behest because he knew how important it was for Carly to have Mia there for the wedding—and he wanted to get married as quickly as possible.

He'd gone to the facility and brought Mia back the minute the program was over. She was his wedding-day surprise for Carly. He'd kept it a secret, pretending that Mia wasn't going to be able to make it because of a last-minute delay, then sprung his surprise that morning.

Carly doubted that she had ever loved Hawk more than she did right this minute. He really was one of a kind. And he was hers.

Mia inspected Carly one last time. The ceremony was almost ready to begin. She caught her lower lip between her teeth and broached a delicate subject. It was now or never.

"I know this probably sounds awful, but would you mind very much if I stayed here for a couple of days?" Before Carly could answer, she quickly added, "It's just until I can figure out where I'm going to go."

"Go?" Carly echoed, confused. "You're not going anywhere. This is your home, Mia. You're going to live right here with us."

Mia laughed and rolled her eyes. "Right. I'm sure that'll make Hawk very happy," she cracked.

"As a matter of fact," Carly informed her, pressing her hand over the butterflies that had suddenly materialized in her stomach, "we've already talked it over, and he's fine with this."

"And what did he say *after* you untied him?" Mia deadpanned.

"I still said 'fine,'" Hawk confirmed, his voice floating in from the hallway.

Mia's eyes widened as she whirled around. She quickly crossed to the door. "Stop!" she cried. "You can't see the bride in her wedding dress before the wedding! It's bad luck!"

But when Hawk walked in the doorway, he had his hand covering his eyes. "I can't see anything," he promised. "See? I've got my hand over my eyes."

"What are you doing here?" Mia asked, peering at him to make sure he hadn't splayed his fingers apart enough to catch a glimpse of Carly.

"Heard you two talking and I came to back up my lovely bride-to-be. You're staying here, Mia," he said with finality. "It'll make us both happy. Besides, I've never had a little sister before. Might be fun," he added with a grin.

Strains of the *Wedding March,* courtesy of Patterson and a portable keyboard he'd brought along—who knew the man could play?—came drifting into the bedroom. "I believe they're playing your song, Carly," Hawk said, still covering his eyes. He turned on his heel, one hand braced on the doorjamb. "I'd better get to that make-shift altar Jeffers and Rosenbloom made for us."

Carly smiled when she thought of the men arguing as they'd worked feverishly to complete the altar where they were going to exchange their vows. "You know some very talented agents."

Hawk laughed. "Yeah, go figure. And they're special agents," he reminded her.

"Yes," Carly wholeheartedly agreed, "they certainly are."

"Go, shoo, get ready," Mia instructed, putting her hands on Hawk's back and gently pushing her almost brother-in-law out of the room.

"Yes, ma'am," Hawk answered obediently. In a moment, he was gone.

Mia gave it to the count of five, then looked at her sister. "Ready?"

Carly took a deep, fortifying breath. "I've been ready for ten years," she confessed.

Mia smiled at her. "Well, then," she said, ushering her sister out of the room, then picking up the edge of

SUSPENSE

Heartstopping stories of intrigue and mystery—
where true love always triumphs.

Harlequin® ROMANTIC

SUSPENSE

COMING NEXT MONTH
AVAILABLE JANUARY 31, 2012

#1691 HIS DUTY TO PROTECT
Black Jaguar Squadron
Lindsay McKenna

#1692 RANCHER'S PERFECT BABY RESCUE
Perfect, Wyoming
Linda Conrad

#1693 THE PRETENDER
Scandals of Sierra Malone
Kathleen Creighton

#1694 AWOL WITH THE OPERATIVE
Jean Thomas

You can find more information on upcoming Harlequin® titles,
free excerpts and more at www.HarlequinInsideRomance.com.

HRSCNM0112

REQUEST YOUR FREE BOOKS!
2 FREE NOVELS PLUS 2 FREE GIFTS!

Harlequin®

ROMANTIC
SUSPENSE

Sparked by Danger, Fueled by Passion.

YES! Please send me 2 FREE Harlequin® Romantic Suspense novels and my 2 FREE gifts (gifts are worth about $10). After receiving them, if I don't wish to receive any more books, I can return the shipping statement marked "cancel." If I don't cancel, I will receive 4 brand-new novels every month and be billed just $4.49 per book in the U.S. or $5.24 per book in Canada. That's a saving of at least 14% off the cover price! It's quite a bargain! Shipping and handling is just 50¢ per book in the U.S. and 75¢ per book in Canada.* I understand that accepting the 2 free books and gifts places me under no obligation to buy anything. I can always return a shipment and cancel at any time. Even if I never buy another book, the two free books and gifts are mine to keep forever.

240/340 HDN FEFR

Name _____
(PLEASE PRINT)

Address _____ Apt. #

City _____ State/Prov. _____ Zip/Postal Code

Signature (if under 18, a parent or guardian must sign)

Mail to the **Reader Service:**

IN U.S.A.: P.O. Box 1867, Buffalo, NY 14240-1867
IN CANADA: P.O. Box 609, Fort Erie, Ontario L2A 5X3

Not valid for current subscribers to Harlequin Romantic Suspense books.

Want to try two free books from another line?
Call 1-800-873-8635 or visit www.ReaderService.com.

* Terms and prices subject to change without notice. Prices do not include applicable taxes. Sales tax applicable in N.Y. Canadian residents will be charged applicable taxes. Offer not valid in Quebec. This offer is limited to one order per household. All orders subject to credit approval. Credit or debit balances in a customer's account(s) may be offset by any other outstanding balance owed by or to the customer. Please allow 4 to 6 weeks for delivery. Offer available while quantities last.

Your Privacy—The Reader Service is committed to protecting your privacy. Our Privacy Policy is available online at www.ReaderService.com or upon request from the Reader Service.

We make a portion of our mailing list available to reputable third parties that offer products we believe may interest you. If you prefer that we not exchange your name with third parties, or if you wish to clarify or modify your communication preferences, please visit us at www.ReaderService.com/consumerschoice or write to us at Reader Service Preference Service, P.O. Box 9062, Buffalo, NY 14269. Include your complete name and address.

HRS11B

Harlequin
Super Romance

Discover a touching new trilogy from
USA TODAY bestselling author

Janice Kay Johnson

Between Love and Duty

As the eldest brother of three, Duncan MacLachlan
is used to being in control and maintaining an
emotional distance; as a police captain it's his job.
But when he meets Jane Brooks, Duncan soon finds
his control slipping away. Together, they fight for a
young boy's future, and soon Duncan finds himself
hoping to build a future with Jane.

Available February 2012

From Father to Son
(March 2012)

The Call of Bravery
(April 2012)

www.Harlequin.com

HSR71758

Louisa Morgan loves being around children.
So when she has the opportunity to tutor bedridden Ellie,
she's determined to bring joy back into the motherless
girl's world. Can she also help Ellie's father open his
heart again? Read on for a sneak peek of

THE COWBOY FATHER

by Linda Ford,
available February 2012 from Love Inspired Historical.

Why had Louisa thought she could do this job? A bubble of self-pity whispered she was totally useless, but Louisa ignored it. She wasn't useless. She could help Ellie if the child allowed it.

Emmet walked her out, waiting until they were out of earshot to speak. "I sense you and Ellie are not getting along."

"Ellie has lost her freedom. On top of that, everything is new. Familiar things are gone. Her only defense is to exert what little independence she has left. I believe she will soon tire of it and find there are more enjoyable ways to pass the time."

He looked doubtful. Louisa feared he would tell her not to return. But after several seconds' consideration, he sighed heavily. "You're right about one thing. She's lost everything. She can hardly be blamed for feeling out of sorts."

"She hasn't lost everything, though." Her words were quiet, coming from a place full of certainty that Emmet was more than enough for this child. "She has you."

"She'll always have me. As long as I live." He clenched his fists. "And I fully intend to raise her in such a way that even if something happened to me, she would never feel like I was gone. I'd be in her thoughts and in her actions every day."

Peace filled Louisa. "Exactly what my father did."

Their gazes connected, forged a single thought about fathers and daughters...how each needed the other. How sweet the relationship was.

Louisa tipped her head away first. "I'll see you tomorrow."

Emmet nodded. "Until tomorrow then."

She climbed behind the wheel of their automobile and turned toward home. She admired Emmet's devotion to his child. It reminded her of the love her own father had lavished on Louisa and her sisters. Louisa smiled as fond memories of her father filled her thoughts. Ellie was a fortunate child to know such love.

Louisa understands what both father and daughter are going through. Will her compassion help them heal—and form a new family? Find out in
THE COWBOY FATHER
by Linda Ford, available February 14, 2012.

Love Inspired Books celebrates 15 years of inspirational romance in 2012! February puts the spotlight on Love Inspired Historical, with each book celebrating family and the special place it has in our hearts. Be sure to pick up all four Love Inspired Historical stories, available February 14, wherever books are sold.

Copyright © 2012 by Linda Ford

SHLIHEXP0212

Rhonda Nelson

SIZZLES WITH ANOTHER INSTALLMENT OF

When former ranger Jack Martin is assigned to
provide security to Mariette Levine, a local pastry
chef, he believes this will be an open-and-shut case.
Yet the danger becomes all too real when Mariette is
attacked. But things aren't always what they seem,
and soon Jack's protective instincts demand he save
the woman he is quickly falling for.

THE KEEPER

**Available February 2012
wherever books are sold.**

www.Harlequin.com

HB79668

Harlequin *Presents*®

USA TODAY bestselling author

Sarah Morgan

brings readers another enchanting story

ONCE A FERRARA WIFE...

When Laurel Ferrara is summoned back to Sicily
by her estranged husband, billionaire
Cristiano Ferrara, Laurel knows things are about
to heat up. And Cristiano's power is a potent
reminder of his Sicilian dynasty's unbreakable rule:
once a Ferrara wife, always a Ferrara wife....

Sparks fly this February

www.Harlequin.com

HP13049

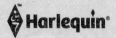

Harlequin®

n●cturne™

NEW YORK TIMES AND *USA TODAY*
BESTSELLING AUTHOR

RACHEL LEE

captivates with another installment of

The Claiming

When Yvonne Dupuis gets a creepy sensation that
someone is watching her, waiting in the shadows,
she turns to Messenger Investigations and finds herself
under the protection of vampire Creed Preston.
His hunger for her is extreme, but with evil lurking
at every turn Creed must protect Yvonne from the
demonic forces that are trying to capture her
and claim her for his own.

CLAIMED BY A VAMPIRE

Available in February wherever books are sold.

HN61876